WISE UP, ALEX

Carrie strode past Alex and Sky and knocked loudly on the door. "We're going in," she said impatiently. "We're *here*, aren't we? Besides, it's going to be funny, remember?"

"Coming!" Amy called from deep inside the house.

Oh, boy, Alex thought. She shifted her feet, gripping her skateboard tightly under her arm. She kept her eyes pinned to her sneakers. She couldn't let Carrie and Sky see how scared she really was. Her palms were sweaty and her heart was rattling like a machine gun.

A moment later the door opened. "Hi, Alex!" Amy sang out. "I'm so glad . . ." Her voice trailed off when her eyes fell on Sky and Carrie.

Alex's insides lurched.

I'm in big, big trouble . . .

M·a·k·i·n·g F·r·i·e·n·d·s

1. Wise up, Alex
2. Cool it, Carrie

Coming soon
3. Face facts, Sky   *November 1997*
4. Grow up, Amy   *December 1997*
5. Go for it, Alex   *January 1998*
6. Tough Luck, Carrie   *February 1998*

All *Making Friends* titles can be ordered at your local bookshop or are available by post from Book Service by Post (tel: 01624 675137).

Making Friends

Wise up, Alex

Kate Andrews

MACMILLAN CHILDREN'S BOOKS

First published 1997 by Macmillan Children's Books
a division of Macmillan Publishers Limited
25 Eccleston Place, London SW1W 9NF
and Basingstoke

Associated companies throughout the world

ISBN 0 330 35120 6

Copyright © Dan Weiss Associates, Inc. 1997
Photography by Jutta Klee

The right of Kate Andrews to be identified as the
author of this work has been asserted by her in accordance
with the Copyright, Designs and Patents Act 1988.

1 3 5 7 9 8 6 4 2

A CIP catalogue record for this book is available from
the British Library

Printed and bound in Great Britain by Mackays of Chatham plc, Kent

The cast of
M·a·k·i·n·g F·r·i·e·n·d·s

Alex

Age: 13

Looks: Light brown hair, blue eyes

Family: Mother died when she was a baby; lives with her dad and her brother Matt, aged 14

Likes: Skateboarding; her family and friends; wearing baggy T-shirts and jeans; being adventurous; letting her feelings show!

Dislikes: People who make fun of her skateboard, her brother or her dad; dressing smart or girly; anything to do with maths or science; dishonesty

Carrie

Age: 13

Looks: Long dark hair – often dyed black! Hazel eyes

Family: Awful! No brothers or sisters; very rich parents who go on about money all the time

Likes: Writing stories; wearing black (drives her mum mad!); thinking deep thoughts; Sky's parents and their awesome houseboat!

Dislikes: Her full name – Carrington; her parents; her mum's choice of clothes; jokes about her hair; computers

Sky

Age: 13

Looks: Light brown skin, dark hair, brown eyes

Family: Crazy! Lives on a houseboat with weird parents and a brother, Leif, aged 8

Likes: Shopping; trendy gear; TV; pop music; talking!

Dislikes: Her parents' bizarre lifestyle; having no money; eating meat

Jordan

Age: 13

Looks: Floppy fair hair, green eyes

Family: Uncomfortable! Four big brothers – all so brilliant at sports he can never compete with them

Likes: Drawing! (especially cartoons); basketball (but don't tell anyone!); playing sax (badly); taking the mickey out of his brothers

Dislikes: Being "baby brother" to four brainless apes; Sky when she starts gossiping

Sam

Age: 13

Looks: Native-American; very dark hair, very dark eyes

Family: Confusing! Both parents are Native-American but have different views on how their kids should look and behave; one sister – Shawna, aged 16

Likes: Skateboarding with Alex; computers (especially surfing the Net); writing for the school paper; goofing around

Dislikes: The way his friends dump their problems on each other; his parents' arguments

Amy

Age: 13

Looks: Sickeningly gorgeous blonde hair; baby blue eyes (yuck!)

Family: Spoilt rotten by her dad, which worries her mum; two big sisters

Likes: Having loads of expensive clothes; making other people feel stupid; Matt (Alex's brother) – she fancies him; being leader of "The Amys" – her bunch of snobby friends

Dislikes: Alex, Carrie and Sky! Looking stupid or childish

Mel

Age: 13

Looks: Black hair, dark eyes

Family: Nice parents who work very hard to do their best for Mel

Likes: Her mum and dad; her friends – but should these be the Amys, or Alex, Carrie and Sky? Standing up for herself; reading horror novels

Dislikes: Amy, when she's rotten to other people; worrying about who are her *real* friends

<u>Alex Wagner's Book of Deep Thoughts</u>

<u>Entry 1</u>

Okay, before I get started, I have to make one thing perfectly clear. This is <u>not</u> a diary. Personally, when I think of diaries, I think of these weird, loner-type girls with names like Irma who collect stuffed animals and always have little bits of cereal stuck in their braces. I don't even have braces. So I just want to set the record straight. That way, in case of an emergency, like if I'm killed in a bizarre skateboarding accident or my brother starts snooping around my room for no reason (yes <u>you</u>, Matt), anyone who finds this notebook will know that Alex Wagner never kept a diary. Got it, people? <u>It's</u> <u>not</u> a <u>diary.</u>

Anyway, the reason I'm writing stuff down in the first place is because tomorrow is the first day of school. And every year I make two lists.

<u>Things I Love About Robert Lowell Middle School</u>
1. The <u>courtyard</u>. It's perfect for

skateboarding. I guess skateboarding is the one thing that I do really well, as far as school goes. Things that I don't do so well include taking math tests and reading poetry out loud in Ms. Lloyd's English class.

2. The bus. The five of us (Carrie, Sky, Sam, Jordan, and me) have been riding Bus #4 ever since the first day of fifth grade. At this point, we pretty much own the backseat.

3. Seattle. Well, actually Robert Lowell is in Ocean's Edge, but that's still closer to Seattle than Taylor Haven is. Taylor Haven is Nowheres-ville. There isn't a whole lot to do except go boating on Puget Sound or hang out at other people's houses. I guess I do like Sky's houseboat, though.

4. Sky's houseboat. Okay, I know it's not part of school, but we always invite ourselves over when school is out. Her parents are totally cool about letting us hang around. I just wish they would stop buying alfalfa sprouts and rice cakes and get some normal snacks.

Things I Hate About Robert Lowell Middle School

1. The food. Most of it tastes like

fricasseed cow manure.

2. Any class having to do with math or science.

3. The fact that nobody seems to believe that a girl can skateboard better than a boy.

4. Ms. Lloyd's beard. I'm serious. She has these whiskers on her chin and one of them is at least half an inch long.

5. Sometimes Brick plays air drums along with the radio while he's driving the bus.

6. Seattle. I know I said I liked it, but it rains too much.

Anyway, those are the lists, and they're always pretty much the same. But tomorrow isn't just any first day. It's the first day of eighth grade. And as everyone knows, being in the eighth grade at Robert Lowell is like being a senior in high school, or the boss of a major company, or the undisputed heavyweight champion of the world. Well, maybe that's pushing it a little. But you get the point. Things will be totally different.

First of all, as of tomorrow, I will be one of the best skaters at Robert Lowell. My only real competition was Mark Sullivan, Jordan's older brother, and he'll be in high school. Anyway, he's a dork, in my humble opinion. (I can write that here because I know he'll never see it.)

And speaking of high school, my older brother will be there, too. That means for the first time in my life, Matt won't be waiting around every corner or yelling at me just because I'm wearing his Supersonics cap.

I guess the best thing about being in the eighth grade is that I'll only have one year left until high school. I know it sounds weird, but when I'm in high school, I think Matt and Dad will finally start thinking of me as a real person. They've always thought of me as a little kid who needs to be watched all the time.

But that's kind of natural, I guess. After all, Dad tries really hard to make up for the fact that I don't have a mom. He always wants to do these activities that he thinks girls and moms are supposed to do together, like go shopping for dresses. Ugh. But it's not even like I miss having a mom or anything. I mean, she died before I was two, so I can't really say . . .

Wait a second. This is starting to sound like a diary, isn't it?

One

"All right, you guys—time to get up! Summer's over!"

Alex cringed at the sound of her father's booming, cheerful voice. *Do you have to put it that way?* she wondered, burying her head under the pillows. There were much better ways of waking people up than telling them that the summer was over. He could have just said, "Rise and shine," or, "Breakfast will be ready in ten minutes—"

"Alex?" He knocked on the door. "Time to get up, honey."

"I know," she croaked. "I hear you. I hear you."

"Just making sure. Don't go back to sleep." His footsteps padded down the stairs. "The bus will be here before you know it."

Alex sat up in bed and ran both hands through her unruly mop of hair, then rubbed

5

the sleep from her eyes. The shades were drawn, but a few thin shafts of sunlight poked through the curtains, casting brilliant spots on her clothing-strewn carpet. She shook her head. She couldn't believe she actually had to go to *school*. She was way too groggy. Hadn't the summer just started?

She stretched, yawning. Her body seemed to be made of stone. Maybe she could just lie back down and rest for another few minutes. . . .

All at once her bedroom door flew open.

"Hey!" she protested. "What the . . ."

Matt was standing in the doorway, frowning. He had obviously just woken up. He was wearing an old T-shirt and boxer shorts—his version of pajamas—and his curly brown hair was a mess. He was holding Alex's skateboard. He dangled it in front of him, as if it were a dead fish.

"Would you mind not leaving this in the hall?" he snapped.

"Would you mind *knocking* first?" she replied.

He shook his head. "Alex, you don't get it," he said. He was using that annoying

6

"I'm-your-older-brother-so-you-better listen-to-me" voice. "I nearly tripped over this. Now how am I supposed to play hoops if I break my leg?"

She grinned. "With crutches?"

"Very funny," he said flatly. He tossed the skateboard onto her floor. It hit the carpet with a loud thump, bounced once, then rolled to a stop next to a pair of baggy black jeans. "Keep this dangerous contraption in here where it belongs."

Alex rolled her eyes. Recently, Matt had started using all these big words, like *contraption*. He must have thought that using big words made him sound smarter. In Alex's opinion, big words just made him sound like a dork. She was about to point that out when she realized something.

Matt had turned to leave—but he wasn't walking back in the direction of his room. He was walking in the direction of the bathroom.

"Don't even think it!" she shrieked, instantly wide awake. She leapt out of bed and dashed into the hall just in time to see the bathroom door slam shut.

"Don't even think what?" he snickered. He turned on the faucet, filling the hall with the muffled sound of rushing water.

"Oh, please," she moaned. She lumbered over to the door and knocked twice. The sleeve of her oversized flannel pajama top flopped listlessly against the wood. "Come on, Matt," she pleaded. "You know that I need to get in there first."

"Why?" he called back, turning the water even higher.

"Because!" she yelled.

"Because *what?* You'll have to do better than that, Alex."

She paused. The truth was that she didn't have a good reason. She just hated going into the bathroom after him. Whenever he went first, the floor got all wet, and the mirror got all steamed up, and she always had to rush. But telling him that wouldn't do any good. Besides, she always left the bathroom in the exact same condition when *she* went first. That was why he had beaten her there in the first place.

"Because the bus will be here soon," she said after a moment. "*You* don't even ride the bus anymore. *You're* in high school now."

"No dice," he replied.

"Well, I'm a girl. And everyone knows that girls need more time in the bathroom than boys."

He laughed. "Give me a break. Girls may need more time, but *you* don't."

She frowned. What on earth was that supposed to mean? "Um, in case you forgot, I *am* a girl," she said.

"Yeah, you're a girl, but you're not a *girl* girl," he answered snidely. "You don't wear makeup or do your hair or any of that stuff. So you don't need any more time in here than I do."

For a moment, Alex just stood there, scowling at the bathroom door. Not a *girl* girl. That had to be the dumbest thing she'd ever heard. So what if she didn't do her hair or put on makeup? That didn't change the simple fact that girls took longer in the bathroom than boys. Anyway, it wasn't as if she were *that* ungirlish.

"Matt, if you don't—"

Matt chuckled. "Use Dad's bathroom." He turned on the shower.

"Hey!" she cried. She began pounding furiously on the door. "I'm not done talking to you yet! Turn that off!"

"Alex?" Mr. Wagner called from downstairs. "Is everything all right up there?"

She hesitated, her fist in midair. "No, not really."

"What's up?" he asked.

Her hand dropped to her side. "Well, Matt won't let me use the bathroom first. He doesn't understand that I'm a *girl* and that *girls* need more time in there than *boys*." She directed the last few words at the door.

"Alex—if he got there first, then he's entitled to use it," her father said patiently. "Why don't you use my bathroom?"

"Fine," she mumbled. She marched down the hall, through her father's room, and into his bathroom. She couldn't believe it. First of all, the only shampoo her father had in there was this ultrapowerful dry scalp stuff that made her hair feel like a clump of seaweed. He didn't even have any conditioner. He didn't even have a *blow-dryer*. How was she supposed to prepare

10

herself for the first day of eighth grade under these conditions?

"Not a *girl* girl," she muttered to herself.

She glanced into the mirror.

Yuck. She looked almost as bad as she felt. Her blue eyes were puffy, her shoulder-length brown hair was stringy, and her skin was colorless. But she always looked terrible in the morning. That was why she needed to use her *own* bathroom.

There was a knock on the door. "Alex?"

"Yeah, Dad?"

"I have an extra bottle of that herbal shampoo you like, in case you want it."

Hmm. She couldn't help but smile. In spite of the fact that he was a boy, her dad *was* pretty smart. She turned and opened the door.

"Thanks," she said.

"No problem." He handed her the bottle. "I wouldn't want your hair looking like mine, you know."

Alex had to smile. No matter how much her father combed his graying brown hair, a few wild tufts always seemed to be sticking up in different directions. In fact, everything

11

about him was kind of thrown together. He never tucked in his shirt and hardly ever bothered wearing shoes around the house. But that was what was cool about him. He was a lot less uptight than a lot of other dads she knew—well, except for maybe Sky's dad, who was a total hippie. Then again, Mr. Wagner never really had to dress up for anything. He never even really had to leave the house. He worked at home on his computer, thinking up ad campaigns.

"Hey, Dad, can I ask you something?" Alex said.

"Of course."

She bit her lip, thinking about precisely how she wanted to word the question. "Do you think that I'm not . . . you know . . . all that *girlish*? I mean, compared to other girls?"

He smiled. "Let me guess. Matt said something."

"Sort of," she admitted.

Mr. Wagner laughed again softly. "Well, whatever Matt said, I'm sure he didn't mean anything by it. He has a lot on his mind, you know. Today is his first day of high school. It's a big change for him."

12

"Oh yeah," she mumbled, lowering her eyes. She hadn't even *thought* of that. For a second, she felt bad she had even made a big deal out of the bathroom stuff in the first place. Matt was probably freaking out. "It's really nothing," she added.

"Hey—if it's any consolation, *I* think you're plenty girlish," he said. His smile grew thoughtful. "You know, it's amazing. The older you get, the more you look like your—"

"Mom," Alex finished quietly. "I know, I know."

There was a brief silence.

Mr. Wagner patted her on the shoulder, then sighed. "Better get ready," he said and headed back downstairs.

Alex stood there alone in the bathroom for a moment.

The older you get, the more you look like your mom. Blah, blah, blah.

How many times had she heard *that* before?

It was funny. Well, maybe *funny* wasn't the word, but her dad had definitely been saying that sort of thing a lot more than usual these days. He always seemed to be telling

13

Alex that she had her mom's hair, or her eyes, or her "button nose," whatever *that* was supposed to mean. But he always sounded a little surprised when he said it. It was as if he were really thinking, deep down: *If you look so much like her, how come you're so* different?

Alex didn't really have an answer for that.

The one thing that Alex really knew for sure about her mother was this: She had been this really gorgeous, really popular woman in Taylor Haven. Everyone said she'd had more friends than any other mom in the neighborhood. She had always been throwing parties and arranging barbeques. She used to love to take people out on the sound in the Wagners' little boat. She had also done a lot of charity work and stuff like that.

And Alex did . . . what, exactly? She rode her skateboard. That was about it.

Maybe her father was trying to tell her something. Maybe he was telling her she should grow up a little. Maybe he was trying to tell her, very simply, that if she *looked* so much like her mom, then maybe she should start *acting* more like her.

But how could she? She was too young to throw big parties. And when it came right down to it, Alex didn't even think they looked all that much alike. Her mom had been tall and glamorous, with long brown hair. She'd worn dresses all the time. Besides, she'd been so much more—well . . . *feminine*. And grown up. *She* had looked like a *"girl* girl."

Maybe Matt was right. Maybe Alex *wasn't* all that girlish.

Then again, she wasn't about to start wearing dresses.

The only people Alex even *knew* who wore dresses were The Amys. And Alex had always been kind of intimidated by them. If any group of girls deserved to be called *"girl* girls," it was The Amys.

In fact, now that she thought about it, the ultrapretty, superpopular Amys had a lot more in common with her own mom than *she* did.

Alex glanced into the mirror again. So what could she do about it? She supposed she could do something totally radical, like leave her skateboard at home. Or not wear Matt's Supersonics cap. After all, she was in eighth grade. Maybe it *was* time to grow up a little. Maybe she needed to stop being so much of a tomboy.

Who am I kidding?

She couldn't leave her skateboard at home. For starters, Sam was going to bring *his* skateboard—and she was totally psyched to skate with him, especially now that Mark Sullivan was gone. And anyway, the baseball cap was an essential part of her wardrobe. Besides, who cared if she was a tomboy? Her friends didn't, and that was all that mattered—*right?*

Two

Carrie Mersel stood at the end of her driveway waiting for the bus. It was a beautiful, crisp fall day—perfect for a first day of school. A strong breeze rustled her black hair. The tall evergreen trees lining Whidbey Road swayed back and forth with each gust of wind. The air was filled with the scent of pine and the salty odor of Puget Sound, which lay just on the other side of the bluff at the end of the Mersels' backyard.

Of course, Carrie always waited for the bus at the end of her driveway—even if it was pouring rain or the air was filled with the smell of uncollected garbage.

There was really only one reason for that. She liked being outside her house a whole lot better than being *inside* it.

For one thing, her parents were in there. For another, the house was ultramodern and done entirely in peach and pink and white. It looked like the deck of the Starship *Enterprise*, only with less places to sit. But that was understandable. Her parents were total freaks about computers and electronic gizmos and *Star Trek: The Next Generation*. In fact, they were total freaks about old TV shows in general.

Actually, her parents were just total freaks. Period.

Carrie's name was a good example. Carrie was short for Carrington—as in Blake Carrington, as in the guy on *Dynasty*.

Dynasty was another old TV show. Even though it had been canceled a long time ago, Carrie's parents couldn't get enough of it. They had videotapes of almost every episode.

"Oh, Carrie?"

Uh-oh. Her mother was calling her from the front steps. Carrie kept her hazel eyes pinned to the road, praying that the bus would turn the corner. *Come on, Brick, step on it—*

"Carrie, honey?" Mrs. Mersel called again. "Can you come here?"

"But the bus will be here any second,"

Carrie yelled back, without turning around.

"It's only eight-thirty, dear. The bus isn't due to arrive until eight thirty-five."

"Maybe it will be early."

"Carrie, *please*."

Carrie finally looked over her shoulder. "What is it?"

"You won't come in?" her mother asked, smiling hopefully.

"No," Carrie replied. From a distance, her mother looked like one of those brand-new, twenty-first-century Barbie dolls. It was amazing. She was wearing this superstylish gray suit, and her shiny blond hair looked fake in the sunlight—just like Barbie's.

Mrs. Mersel took a step forward. "Well, honey, it's just that your father and I were talking. And here's the thing. Do you really think it's appropriate to dress all in black on the first day of a new school year?"

"Yes," she answered.

"Are you sure?"

Carrie nodded. Of course she was sure. She had spent almost an hour carefully picking her outfit: a long black skirt, a plain black T-shirt, a black sweater, and black combat boots. All of it matched her black knapsack. And her black nail polish. It was perfect.

Her mother let out an anxious little laugh. "Look, dear, I know we agreed to let you dye your hair black. And I'm not going to back out of that agreement. But don't you think the rest of your total presentation should be, you know, a little more positive?"

Carrie shook her head. "No, not really."

Mrs. Mersel's smile faltered. "But honey, none of your friends have such a . . . well, *grim* sense of fashion. What about Skyler? She's always got these cute, bright little—"

"I'm not Skyler, Mom," Carrie interrupted.

"Look, Carrie." Her mother's voice grew firm. "Remember our little talk? Remember how you told us you were going to work on improving your attitude. . . ."

Thankfully, her voice was drowned out by the familiar roar of Robert Lowell Middle School Bus #4. A second later, it lurched around the corner onto Whidbey Road and screeched to a halt in front of the Mersels' driveway. The door squeaked open.

"Bye, Mom!" Carrie yelled.

"Carrie, wait—do you have my new cell phone number . . . ?"

But Carrie had already dashed onto the bus. She let out a huge sigh of relief as the door closed. *Just in time*, she thought. She gave Brick the customary first-of-the-year high five.

"Cool hair," he said in his gravelly voice.

For the first time all morning, Carrie smiled. "Thanks, Brick."

Unlike her mother, Brick had excellent taste.

"Hey, Carrie," a girl's voice sang out. "What happened to you this morning? Did you fall into a tar pit?"

A few kids laughed.

Carrie whirled around.

Amy Anderson, perhaps the most heinous creature at Robert Lowell, was sitting in the front seat, gazing up at her with a big phony smile. Aimee Stewart and Mel Eng—the other two "Amys"—were sitting right behind her. Carrie sneered. It figured Amy would sit in the front seat on the first day of school. That way, she was impossible to avoid. Everbody would be forced to stare at her long blond hair and her tight

21

blue T-shirt and notice how much her chest had grown over the summer.

"You know, I've never been able to figure out why your jokes are so dumb," Carrie said. She tapped a black fingernail against her chin. "But now I've got it. Your T-shirts are too tight. They're cutting off the blood flow to your brain."

Amy didn't say anything. She just kept right on smiling, as if she hadn't heard.

Carrie smiled back, then marched down the aisle. Alex, Jordan, and Sam were already waiting in their old seat—the long seat at the very back. For a second, she wondered where Matt was. And then she remembered. Matt was in high school. He was a lucky guy, now that she thought about it. He never had to see Amy Anderson again.

"What did Amy say?" Alex whispered as Carrie flopped down between her and Jordan.

"Nothing worth repeating," Carrie stated. She glanced out the window. The bluish gray expanse of Puget Sound came into view as the bus began to bounce down the short, sloping hill toward the Taylor Haven peninsula and Sky's houseboat, which was the last stop before school.

"You know, I wonder if Brick would let us take a vote to kick The Amys off the bus this year," Carrie said, half to herself.

"Oh, come on," Alex said. "They're not *that* bad."

"Yeah," Jordan agreed. He brushed a lone strand of his scraggly blond bangs out of his green eyes and grinned. "I mean, look at it this way: They're never boring."

"Boring?" Carrie muttered. "Yeah, well, getting your teeth pulled isn't boring, either. But it's not like I want to do *that* every single day."

As far as she was concerned, The Amys were about as close to pure evil as three people could get. The only things they were missing were pointy hats and broomsticks. But people actually *looked up* to them—just because they wore cool clothes and supposedly did cool stuff, like chase after high school guys. Whoopee.

"Seriously, Carrie," Alex said after a minute. "What's so bad about The Amys, anyway?"

Carrie raised her eyebrows. "You want me to give you the long version or the short version?"

Alex fidgeted with her Supersonics cap, then turned it backward, which was what she always did when she was uncomfortable. She knew perfectly well what was so bad about The Amys. They were always putting people down. *Especially* Carrie.

"I mean, they're not *all* bad," Alex added quietly.

"They're nice to *you*," Carrie said, grinning. "But that's because they're all in love with Matt."

"No they *aren't*," Alex mumbled. "Anyway, they do some good things. Last year, Amy Anderson worked on the school food drive for that homeless shelter in Seattle. Remember?"

Carrie had to laugh. "Alex, give me a break. We *all* did that."

"Yeah, but she organized it," Alex pointed out.

"I bet the only reason she did was to show off and make herself look like some do-gooder," Carrie said.

"I don't think Amy was necessarily trying to show off," Alex said quietly. "My mom did the same kind of thing once, too. And I know *she* wasn't trying to show off."

Oops. Carrie swallowed. No wonder Alex had been sticking up for Amy. She glanced at Jordan and Sam. They were both staring uncomfortably at their laps.

"Speaking of showing off, Alex—you got any new tricks up your sleeve?" Sam asked, thankfully changing the subject. "You know, skating-wise?"

Alex shrugged. "Not really."

"Come on," he teased. He glanced at her skateboard, which was resting under her feet. "You gotta have *something*. You're the king of the courtyard."

"Yeah," Jordan chimed in. "Especially now that my brother's gone."

Alex frowned slightly. "The *king* of the courtyard?" she asked.

Jordan and Sam glanced at each other.

Carrie peered at Alex closely. For some reason, Alex was starting to look a little upset. *Something* was obviously bothering her—something other than the way Carrie was ragging on The Amys. "Hey, Alex—what's wrong?" she asked.

"Nothing," Alex stated. She pulled her baseball cap around so it faced forward again.

Carrie shook her head. "Alex, you *know* you're a really lousy liar, don't you?" she said gently.

Alex opened her mouth, then closed it. She gave the three of them a hesitant look. "Promise you won't laugh?"

Jordan chuckled. "Alex, you know that whenever somebody says, 'Promise you won't laugh,' you're going to laugh—"

Carrie nudged him in the ribs to shut him up. "Ignore him, Alex. What is it?"

"You have to promise," Alex insisted.

Carrie nodded as solemnly as she could manage. "We promise."

Alex took a deep breath. "Well, it's just . . . I mean, I'm sick of the way people talk to me like I'm some kind of tomboy. Like, I wouldn't be *king* of the courtyard, right? I'd be *queen* of the courtyard."

Carrie held on for as long as she could, but finally she started cracking up. That was about the *last* thing she would have expected

Alex to say. Alex was always going on about how there was no difference at all between girls and boys when it came to skateboarding.

Alex tugged at her cap and pulled it low over her eyes. "Look, just forget it," she mumbled.

Carrie finally managed to get a grip on herself. She shook her head. "No, no, I'm sorry. It's just . . ."

"You *do* think of me as a tomboy," Alex finished.

"I didn't say that," Carrie said. "But look at it this way. I mean, you have to admit, you *look* like a tomboy. You're wearing a Supersonics hat—"

"*And* you're carrying a skateboard," Jordan added. "*And* you're wearing a T-shirt that says No Fear. *And* you're wearing baggy jeans." He paused, then grinned. "Now why would anyone think you were a tomboy?"

"*See?*" Alex moaned.

"But since when have you even *cared* about looking like a tomboy?" Carrie asked.

"I *don't* care," Alex said, not very convincingly.

Carrie looked concerned. "Um . . . you

27

aren't going insane or anything, are you? It's only the first day of school. This kind of identity crisis isn't supposed to happen until Christmas, at least."

"*Nooo*," Alex said.

"Good. I was worried there for a sec." Carrie settled back into her seat. Even though she was only joking, Alex's little speech really *had* made her sort of nervous. Carrie honestly wouldn't know what to do if Alex stopped wearing baggy jeans and that green cap. It would be the same as if *she* herself suddenly stopped wearing only black—or if Sky's parents suddenly stopped being hippies.

Some things were just never supposed to change.

Skyler Foley's Eighth-Grade Resolutions

First of all, everybody has to stop coming over all the time. We'll just have to start going to the mall more often. I can't take the stress of having people in my house anymore. My parents have lost their minds. They are _totally_ insane.

I mean, yesterday, I walked in the door at four in the afternoon—a perfectly normal time of day—and the whole boat was filled with incense smoke. It reeked. I could barely see anything. My dad said he had burned some eggplant and was trying to get rid of the smell. Now how are you supposed to get rid of a bad smell with something that smells even _worse?_ I'm just glad that nobody else was there to witness it.

So that's my first resolution: more mall time, less home time.

Second of all, I'm going to do my own

grocery shopping. See, I have to bring my own lunch to school this year because the cafeteria food prices went up. I'm kind of glad in a way, though. Now I get to choose my own menu. The vegetarian menu at Robert Lowell is <u>so</u> lame. All they serve is stuff like mashed potatoes and steamed carrots. And once I found a piece of Yankee pot roast in my rice. It looked like a little dog turd. How did it even get there? I could have actually <u>eaten</u> it if I wasn't looking. Eww! I can't think about it anymore—it's too gross.

Third of all, I'm going to invite myself over to Carrie's every Thursday night to watch <u>Friends.</u> I've given up trying to convince my parents to get a TV.

But I'm also going to try to read more, too. Really. If that makes any sense.

Three

"Ohmm. Ohmm. Ohmm. . . ."

Skyler Foley paced around the tiny kitchen in a frenzy, trying to remember if she had packed everything. Unfortunately, she'd spent most of the morning debating what to do with her frizzy brown hair. In the end, she decided to just pull it up in a ponytail. She kind of liked how her hair looked slicked back. Her dark brown eyes seemed bigger, somehow.

Then, of course, she'd spent another twenty minutes figuring out what to wear. A good color scheme was important for the first day of school. So she had chosen a green T-shirt and a pair of brown corduroys that went well with the natural mocha complexion of her skin. All in all, she felt pretty decent about her outfit.

"Ohmm . . ."

Now she just needed to get the *rest* of her life together. Her eyes kept darting out the window and up the long wooden dock to Pike's Way, the one narrow road that connected Taylor Haven to Ocean's View. The bus was going to be here any second. She hated running late, but she never seemed to be able to do anything about it.

"Ohmm. Ohmm. Ohmm. . . ."

All right, what was she forgetting? She ran over the list in her mind for about the thousandth time: notebook, pencils, tomato juice, banana, falafel sandwich. . . . But it was impossible to concentrate with her mom and dad chanting in the the main cabin.

"Ohmm. Ohmm—"

"Hey!" she shouted. "Will you cut that out!"

There was a pause. "What, honey?" came her dad's sleepy voice.

"I said be quiet!" she answered crossly. "I can't even hear myself *think!*"

"Sorry, Sky," he said with a little chuckle. "We were deep into the first stage."

The first stage of what? she wondered. But she knew better than to ask. It definitely had to do with some new form of meditation or something. And whatever it was, she didn't need to hear about it, especially right now when . . .

Just then, she heard the sound of a horn honking.

"Argh!"

After one last frantic look around the kitchen, she scooped her book bag off the table and dashed through the main cabin toward the door. Her parents were sitting crosslegged on the floor along with her eight-year-old brother, Leif, who was lucky enough to have another whole week of summer vacation. They looked like they were acting out a scene in some bad sixties movie. They were all in their pajamas, with their eyes closed and their backs perfectly straight. Sky just hoped they were sitting low enough so that nobody would be able to see them.

"Bye, everyone!" she called.

Before they could answer, she was out the door and running down the dock toward the big yellow bus.

"What's up, Brick?" She gave him a high five as she climbed on board, then hurried toward the backseat.

"So, what's up?" she asked as she sat down. Her gaze swept across the faces of Carrie, Alex, Jordan, and Sam. "Did I miss anything exciting?"

Jordan exchanged a quick glance with the others. "Uh . . . Sky?" he said. "We haven't even gotten to *school* yet."

"I know, I know—but good stuff always happens on the bus. Especially on the first day."

"Well, let's see," Carrie replied, lowering her voice. "Oh yeah." She jerked her head up the aisle toward Amy Anderson. "Her Royal Coolness told me she doesn't like my wardrobe."

Sky frowned. "Amy? What did she say?"

"Nothing really," Carrie replied breezily. "Just that she doesn't quite go for the goth-rock look. Or something along those lines."

Sky shook her head. Still, she wasn't very surprised. Amy Anderson seemed to have an allergic reaction to anyone who didn't shop at the same hip, overpriced stores where *she* shopped. Luckily, Sky somehow always managed to pass the test.

"Hey—don't look so bummed," Carrie said quietly, patting her shoulder. "If Amy Anderson doesn't like my clothes, I know I must be doing *something* right."

Sky laughed. "So what else happened?"

"Alex freaked out earlier," Jordan announced. "She had some kind of identity crisis. But I think it passed before there was any permanent damage."

"Identity crisis?" Sky smiled. Now *this* was good. "Wow. Sounds major."

"It *wasn't* an identity crisis," Alex groaned. "It's not like I even *care* or anything."

"Care about what?" Sky asked.

"She's worried that people think she's a tomboy," Sam explained.

"Really?" Sky glanced at Alex in confusion. "Well, you *are* a tomboy. I mean, aren't you?"

Alex made a face. "That's exactly what I'm talking about."

"Well, let's do something about it," Sky said brightly.

"Like what?" Alex asked. "Get me an entirely knew wardrobe?"

"Exactly!" Sky exclaimed. "See, today after school we go to the mall and pick out all these awesome clothes, and then we go to Carrie's house and give you a makeover, and—"

"Whoa, whoa," Carrie interrupted, raising her hands. "Slow down. We are *not* going to my house this afternoon."

"And we are *not* giving me a makeover," Alex added.

Sky blinked. "Why not?"

"Because makeovers are the lamest things on the planet," Alex replied matter-of-factly.

"How can you say all that? You've never even tried one." Sky sighed. "Besides, everybody knows that makeovers change lives. They always talk about it in *Seventeen*."

"Look, makeovers do *not* change lives," Alex said. "Besides, how would you know? You've never had one, either."

Sky shook her head. "Yeah, but that's only because I'm not . . . you know . . ." She paused and began twirling a lock of her curly brown hair absently around her forefinger. What was she trying to say, exactly?

"Tomboyish?" Alex prompted.

Sky shrugged, smiling as innocently as she could manage. "Bingo."

"Well, the mall is totally out," Carrie stated.

"We're going to *your* house this afternoon."

"Oh yeah?" Sky asked. "Says who?"

Carrie sighed. "Sky—we *always* go to your house."

Sky wracked her brains for some kind of comeback, but there wasn't any. It was true. Everybody had been coming over to her house for as long as she could remember—and they would probably keep coming over until they were all eighty years old.

"Maybe we should just go somewhere totally different for once," Alex suggested.

"Like where?" Sky asked hopefully.

Alex shrugged. "I don't know. Just as long as it's someplace where you can't give me a makeover. We can talk about it at lunch."

"That's a good idea," Carrie agreed.

Sky nodded. That *was* a good idea. That was perfect, in fact. Talking about it at lunch would give her all morning to think up new and brilliant ways all of them could enrich their lives by going to the mall.

Unless, of course, something better came up.

Four

"Are you going to finish that?" Jordan reached across Sam to point at the remainder of Carrie's lunch.

"Be my guest." She picked up her plate and handed it to Jordan, who immediately polished off the leftovers.

"Jordan, that is so gross!" Sky looked disgusted.

"Some things never change," Sam observed.

Last year, the six of them—including Matt—had chosen the round table near the big glass window that looked out onto the courtyard. Seventh- and eighth-graders ate later than the lower grades and were allowed to choose their own seats.

It was almost as if summer vacation had never happened, Carrie thought. Well, except for the fact that Matt was gone. But last year they'd sat at the same table, and today it seemed as if Sky had just picked up the conversation where she had left off last June.

" . . . but you can skateboard in the parking lot," Sky was whining to Alex. "*I'll* go in and shop—and *you* just wait outside."

"You're not going shopping for me, Sky," Alex said firmly. "And that's that."

"Okay, what if we just go and *look* at stuff?" Sky persisted.

Here we go again. Carrie's gaze wandered out to the courtyard. It was filled with fifth- and sixth-graders. They were all running around and screaming wildly. A thin swatch of clear sky was barely visible over the opposite wall of the school building. Why couldn't summer vacation have lasted another week, like when they were all younger? Today would be such a perfect day to take the Wagners' little motorboat out on the sound. . . .

"Hey, cut it out!"

A high-pitched shriek broke into her thoughts. It was followed by a loud giggle. "Come on," Amy Anderson's voice pleaded. "Leave me alone. I'm *serious*."

Carrie glanced in the direction of the commotion. Johnny Bates and Chris

Tanzell—two meatheads who reminded her of Jordan's older brothers—were hovering around Amy, trying to tickle her. Aimee Stewart and Mel Eng were sitting at the same table, egging them on.

The entire cafeteria was staring at them.

Amy threw her head back and squirmed. She was laughing like a maniac. "I'm serious!" she repeated loudly enough so that it echoed across the whole room.

"She really looks serious, doesn't she?" Carrie muttered sarcastically.

No one said anything. Jordan and Sam both had dumb looks on their faces—like they wouldn't mind tickling Amy themselves. It was too stomach turning to contemplate. Even Alex was staring at The Amys as if she were in some kind of trance.

"Earth to Alex—come in, Alex," Carrie said, cupping her hands over her mouth so that her voice sounded like a walkie-talkie.

Alex didn't respond.

Sam started laughing. "Looks like we've lost all contact."

Finally, Alex blinked. "Huh?" she said, shaking her head.

"I thought we lost you there for a second," Carrie said, letting her hands drop.

"Sorry," she mumbled.

"What's on your mind?" Sky asked curiously.

Alex shrugged. "Nothing, really. I was . . . I was just thinking about something my dad said this morning." She laughed once. "I don't know why I started thinking about that." She pulled her baseball cap out of her back pocket and put it on her head, then stood up and looked at Sam. "Hey—you want to go to the courtyard?"

Sam nodded eagerly. "Yeah. I'm psyched to show you my new board."

Jordan glanced at the big clock on the far wall of the cafeteria. It was only twelve-fifty. "You know, lunch isn't over yet," he said. "Aren't you guys supposed to wait until one?"

"Come on, Jordan," Sky said with a mischievous little grin. "Leave them alone. They just want to go . . . 'skateboarding.'" She dragged the last word out and made little quotation marks in the air.

"And what's *that* supposed to mean?" Alex demanded.

"Oh, nothing," Sky replied nonchalantly.

Alex and Sam frowned at the same time. Then they both snatched their trays off the table and marched toward the kitchen without another word.

"Bye, guys," Sky said. She raised her eyebrows suggestively at Jordan and Carrie. "Serious couple vibes," she whispered.

Carrie couldn't help but smirk. Sky was always trying to entertain herself with made-up gossip.

Jordan glanced at Sam and Alex. "Well, at least I don't think Alex is too worried about being a tomboy anymore," he said after a minute. "She's back to normal, wouldn't you say?"

"I hope so," Carrie said. She was still glaring at Amy Anderson. "Maybe that means she'll finally realize that in fact The Amys *were* sent here by Satan."

"Hey!" Jordan said suddenly. "That reminds me. Speaking of The Amys, I have something I want to show you."

He reached down under his chair and

unzipped his book bag, then yanked out a big drawing pad.

"What's that?" Carrie asked.

"It's the Amys." he said. "Just something I sketched in math class."

43

"So what do you think?" Jordan asked.

Carrie glanced up at him. "I love it," she said. She smiled broadly. "You're gonna make a million bucks one day, you know that?"

Jordan opened his mouth like he was going to say something, only no sound came out.

"Jordan—are you blushing?" Sky asked with a big grin.

He immediately frowned. "No," he stated.

She stared at him dramatically. "It looks like you are to me." She glanced at Carrie.

Carrie rolled her eyes. If Jordan knew what was good for him, he'd leave, too. She knew that tone of Sky's all too well. It meant that she was on the prowl for more "couple vibes." And there definitely *weren't* "couple vibes" between her and Jordan.

"Hey—you know what we should do?" Carrie suddenly announced. Ignoring Sky, she lowered her voice and leaned across the table toward Jordan. "We should post this up on the big bulletin board outside the front office."

Jordan reached for the the pad and tugged it out of her hands. "I don't know. . . ."

"Why not?" Carrie asked.

"Uh—I'm just not ready to share my work with the rest of the world," Jordan said. "I think I'll just keep it in here," he added, shoving the pad back into his book bag.

Carrie sighed disappointedly. "That's too bad," she said. "You're really talented. You should be proud of your work."

She hoped Sky wouldn't notice that Jordan's face was starting to turn pink again. But Sky was fidgeting restlessly in her chair. "So . . . Carrie, do you think we can talk Alex into going to the mall today?"

Carrie looked at Jordan and rolled her eyes. Yep—some things never change.

Five

"Meet you outside in two minutes," Alex said as she and Sam deposited their trays in the kitchen at the back of the cafeteria. "I just gotta go get my skateboard."

"Yeah," Sam mumbled. "Me too." He looked at her one last time, then scurried off toward the set of double doors that led to the boys' lockers.

Alex frowned. Sky's silly little comment had obviously made him really uncomfortable. It was so ridiculous. Just because Sam had taken up skateboarding last year, Sky had gotten it into her head that he had a crush on her or something. They were *friends*. After all, they had known each other since they were six, right? He was more like a brother than anything else.

Alex had to admit that Sam *was* very cool, though—at least as far as guys at

Robert Lowell were concerned. He was really funny, too. And . . . well, he was sort of cute, not that she even cared or anything. He had these big black eyes and straight black hair and incredibly soft-looking skin.

But so what if he was cute? It didn't matter one bit. If Sky wanted to imagine that anyone in their little group had a crush going on, she should try Jordan and Carrie. *Not* her and Sam.

She sighed and began heading toward the set of double doors on the other side of the cafeteria—the ones that led to the girls' lockers.

"Stop it!" Amy Anderson was yelling. "Come on!"

Amy was still being tickled by those two guys.

Alex kept her head down as she passed their table. She just couldn't stand to look over there anymore. Watching Amy all during lunch had made her really, really depressed. She couldn't stop thinking about how much Amy had in common with Alex's own mom. They were both pretty. They were both fun loving. They were both "*girl* girls." They were both everything that Alex wasn't. . . .

"This is the *last* time," Amy gasped. "I mean it. I'm going to—" The rest of her words were lost in a fit of laughter.

Alex stole one last quick peek at Amy before pushing open one of the two big double doors. Then she let it slam behind her. She began the long, slow march down the hall to her locker. But she could still hear Amy giggling.

She shook her head. Above all else, Amy and Alex's mom were both *popular*.

Amy was the kind of person who was *always* surrounded by people. She was *always* having the time of her life. That's what people had said about Alex's mom, too. Not that Alex would ever want to be mauled by a bunch of dumb boys, but still . . . whenever there was something wild and crazy and attention-grabbing going on, Amy Anderson was always sure to be right in the middle of it.

And until this moment, Alex had always considered herself to be pretty popular, too. She'd never really even given it much thought. She definitely wasn't *unpopular*—

"Oh, no, you don't!" Amy cried.

Alex jumped. The double doors slammed. She turned around to see Amy bolting down the hall. She stopped in front of Alex and bent over, gasping for breath.

Alex just stared at her.

"Do you think Chris and Johnny will come in here?" Amy asked, panting.

Alex looked around. Was Amy talking to *her*? She must have been. The hall was completely empty except for the two of them.

"Uh . . . I don't know," she said awkwardly.

"Oh, well. It doesn't matter." Amy stood up straight and gave Alex a broad smile. "You know—it's lucky I ran into you."

Alex frowned. "It *is*?"

"Yeah." Amy nodded. "I've been meaning to talk to you all day. Aimee and Mel and I were wondering if you wanted to come over to my house this afternoon and watch *Days of Our Lives* with us."

Alex blinked. *Wait a second.* This had to be some sort of joke.

"Can you?" Amy asked.

Alex's jaw dropped slightly. "What?"

Amy laughed. "It's not a trick question."

For a moment, Alex half expected to suddenly wake up and find herself at home in bed. This was unreal. The Amys watched *Days of Our Lives* in private. Only a very select few were ever invited to join them. *Ever.* And Alex was not one of them. Being asked to watch *Days of Our Lives* at Amy Anderson's house was like being asked to join a secret cult or the CIA or something.

"Well?" Amy prodded.

Finally, Alex managed to get a grip on herself—at least enough to say one word.

"Why?"

"Why?" Amy laughed again. "Because I *want* you to."

Alex didn't say anything. Why did Amy Anderson suddenly want Alex to start hanging out with her *now*, after three whole years? It didn't make any sense.

"So what do you say?"

Alex unconsciously reached for the bill of her Supersonics cap and clutched it—as if it would somehow help her from losing her balance. "I . . . uh, well," she stammered.

"Come on," Amy urged.

"Well, sure," Alex said, forcing a smile.

"Great! I'll see you at four?"

"I'll see you at four," Alex echoed hollowly. She felt as if she were listening to someone else answer the question.

"You know where my house is, right?" Amy asked.

Alex nodded. "It's the big white house on Pacific Drive, at the top of the hill—"

The bell rang, cutting her off. A moment later, a swarm of kids flooded out of the cafeteria and into the hall. Johnny Bates and Chris Tanzell were leading the pack. They broke into a wild run when they saw Amy.

"Oh, boy," Amy murmured. "Gotta go!"

Before Alex could say anything more, Amy disappeared around the corner at the other end of the hall. Alex suddenly found herself being jostled by Chris and Johnny, then by a bunch of girls all trying to get to their lockers before recess.

She shook her head.

It had all happened so quickly. *Too* quickly.

Had she *really* been invited to Amy Anderson's house?

Yes. She really had.

A strange, tingling excitement swept over her. She couldn't believe it.

It was as if the whole planet had flipped upside down in a matter of seconds. She had been wanting to do something totally radical—something totally *untomboyish*—ever since this morning. And here was the perfect opportunity. It was almost too good to be true. She couldn't *think* of anything more girlish than watching *Days of Our Lives* with The Amys. Nope. She nearly laughed out loud. That was about as girlish as it got. . . .

"Um, Alex?"

Alex looked up. Carrie and Sky were coming toward her through the crowd.

Carrie shot a quick glance at Sky. "What's up?" she asked, grinning. "You look like you just won the lottery."

Alex just smiled. "You guys are going to *freak* when I tell you what just happened," she said. "I mean, *freak*."

Six

"Are you *serious?*" Carrie whispered.

Alex nodded excitedly. "Yup."

"And you actually agreed to go?" Carrie asked. She was shocked.

Alex paused. "Well . . . yeah." She fiddled with her baseball cap, then looked at the floor. "Why shouldn't I?"

Carrie's face fell. This was *terrible.* Then again, this was Amy Anderson. Only Amy would start her morning by insulting Carrie, then turn around and invite one of Carrie's best friends over to watch *Days of Our Lives.* She might as well have smacked Carrie in the face.

"Look—she invited all of us," Alex stated. "And I told her we were all coming. So it would be kind of rude not to go, right?"

Carrie didn't answer. Something about Alex's tone made her slightly suspicious. She had spoken a little too loudly and a little too quickly. "Are you *sure* she invited us?" Carrie asked.

Alex threw her hands up in the air. "Of course I'm sure!"

"But I thought we were going to *Sky's* house," Carrie murmured.

Alex sighed. "That's the whole point. We couldn't decide *what* we wanted to do. Besides, *you* agreed with me that we should do something completely different. So here's our chance."

Carrie hung her head. *Great*, she thought miserably. It figured her own words would come back to haunt her. She looked at Sky. Why wasn't she saying anything? Couldn't she see that Alex had lost her mind?

"Sky?" Alex asked. "What do you think? You're pysched to go, too, right?"

"I don't know . . . ," Sky said uncertainly.

"You don't *know?*" Carrie cried. "I thought you wanted to go to the mall!"

Sky didn't answer right away. She began twirling her finger in her hair. Carrie knew that was a bad sign. It meant she was going to say something she knew Carrie wouldn't want to hear.

"Carrie—I never thought I'd be the one to say this, but the mall can wait," Sky said. "Seriously. I mean, a chance like this comes around like once every million years or so. We'll be among the very few to actually *see* The Amys watch *Days of Our Lives*. It's like seeing the Loch Ness monster or something. Do you know how much gossip there is about these little get-togethers? It could fill the entire *library.*"

Carrie shook her head. "Well, you guys have fun," she muttered. "There's no way *I'm* going."

Alex sighed. "Carrie—"

"I'm serious," she interrupted. Why were they even having this conversation? *Anything* was better than watching *Days of Our Lives* with The Amys, wasn't it? Even watching *Dynasty* with her mom was better. At least there was only *one* of her mom.

"Look, Carrie—if it's lame, we'll leave," Alex promised. "I swear."

"Well, what about the little run-in I had with Amy on the bus this morning?" Carrie asked. "Don't you think it's strange that she suddenly wants me to start watching soap operas with her?"

"Carrie, Amy *always* puts people down," Alex replied. "She doesn't mean anything by it." She bit her lip. "Otherwise, she wouldn't have invited you, right?"

"I don't know," Carrie said doubtfully.

"Aren't you sort of curious about what goes on at Amy Anderson's house?" Sky asked.

"Well, yeah, sure—a *little*," Carrie admitted. "But I'm also curious about what goes on in the boys' locker room. That doesn't mean I want to *go*."

Alex laughed. "Look—what's the worst thing that can happen? It bites, and we leave. No harm done."

"One time couldn't hurt," Sky added. She smiled slightly. "And the truth is, it might actually be kind of funny."

"Funny?" Carrie asked. But much to her own surprise, she also cracked a little smile. The idea of the six of them all hanging out and watching a soap opera *was* pretty funny, now that she thought about it. It was absurd. What would they do when it was over—bake cookies together?

Finally, she sighed. "I don't know. If I'm

looking for laughs, I can always watch *Evil Dead II.*"

Sky grinned. "Come on. It won't be *that* bad."

"How would you know?" Carrie asked. "Maybe Amy wants to use us as a human sacrifice or something. Maybe she lost a bet with the devil and owes him three souls."

"Well, that would be perfect then," Sky said matter-of-factly. "You could use the experience as inspiration for one of your stories."

Carrie shook her head. Sky was the only person in the world who could take human sacrifice and try to turn it into a selling point.

Still, deep down, Carrie *was* sort of curious about the whole thing. The Amys must have had a reason for inviting them over—a *real* reason.

"So what do you say?" Alex asked.

Carrie's gaze shifted between the two of them. "I don't know . . ."

"It's the chance of a lifetime," Alex prodded.

Carrie smirked. "Right."

"And we'll leave if it's lame," she repeated.

She hesitated. "You promise?" she said, unable to believe she was even *asking* the question.

"Promise," they both said at the same time.

Carrie knew it was pointless to fight them on this. They would just keep badgering her until she agreed. "All right," she mumbled grudgingly.

"Great," Alex said quickly. "So, after school we'll go to Sky's house and then head over to Amy's, okay?"

Before they could answer, Alex dashed for the door that opened onto the courtyard.

Carrie glanced at Sky. "Where's *she* going?"

Sky shrugged. "Skateboarding, remember?" Her face grew serious. "Look, Carrie—are you sure you're okay with this?"

Carrie nodded. But she didn't trust herself to speak. The truth was that she *wasn't* okay with it. She just didn't want to disappoint them.

As far as she was concerned, they were all making a big, big mistake.

<u>Alex Wagner's Book</u> <u>of</u> <u>Deep Thoughts</u>

<u>Entry 2</u>

Well, I must say, the first day of eighth grade is definitely <u>not</u> turning out the way I expected.

I didn't think in a million years I'd be going to Amy Anderson's house this afternoon.

I didn't think I'd lie to my two best friends, either.

I guess Carrie was wrong about what she said on the bus this morning. I'm a better liar than she thought.

Wow. It's kind of scary.

The thing is, though, I sort of <u>had</u> to tell Carrie and Sky they were invited. I didn't want them to feel left out. And to be honest, I'd be way too nervous to go to Amy's on my own. Plus, Carrie and Sky would totally rag on me if I did.

I just really, really hope Amy doesn't get mad.

But what's the worst that can happen? It's not like I even <u>like</u> The Amys that much or anything. It's just that I'm . . . well, like Sky said, I'm curious about them.

The Amys have pretty much been the coolest girls in our class since the fifth grade. I mean, look at it this way: They're the only three girls at school who have an actual <u>title</u>. Nobody ever gave Sky, Carrie, and me a title. We're not known as The Whatevers. Of course, none of us have the same first name or anything, but still, it's different. The Amys have this weird kind of power over people.

As far as lies go, I really don't think it was all <u>that</u> bad telling Carrie and Sky they were invited. Amy knows the three of us hang out together. It could have been worse. It wasn't a total lie. Amy didn't say that they <u>weren't</u> invited.

If I can actually be friends with Amy, I think my last year at Robert Lowell Middle School is going to be much, much better. If <u>she</u> thinks of me as someone she can be friends with, I think other people might start thinking of me as more of a regular girl. I know people think of me as normal and everything, but after I hang out with Amy, maybe they won't think of me as so much of a . . . you know. A tomboy.

And that would be fine by me.

Seven

By the time the final bell rang, Sky's brain seemed to have shrunk to a single, solitary thought.

Carrie doesn't want to go to Amy's house. We're forcing her to go.

She'd only really begun to think about it after recess was over. And pretty soon after that, she couldn't think about anything else. She couldn't even pay attention in class. She felt too guilty. So what if she was curious about The Amys and *Days of Our Lives*? It didn't mean she and Alex had to drag Carrie along with them—especially after the way Amy had put Carrie down this morning. No, they should have never agreed to go in the first place.

There's only one thing to do, she thought determinedly as she made her way to the semicircular drive in front of the school building. *I just have to talk Alex out of going. None of us will go. We have to stick together—*

"Hey, um, Sky?"

Sky glanced behind her. Jordan was standing on the front steps, calling her name. Carrie, Alex, and Sam were all standing around him, staring at her.

Her lips curled in a puzzled frown. "What?" she asked.

He smiled. "Uh . . . do you realize you're about to get run over?"

Sky looked around. It was true. She had been so distracted that she'd walked right into the middle of the driveway. Bus #4 was pulling up to the front steps. Unfortunately, she couldn't move. Her legs seemed to have frozen solid.

Honk!

A loud horn blast snapped her out of her stupor.

"Jeez," she muttered. She dashed back to where the rest of them were standing.

"Watch it there!" Brick shouted, opening the door. He grinned crookedly. "I don't want to kill anybody. I *need* this job."

Sky managed a weak little laugh. "Ha, ha, ha."

"Are you all right?" Carrie asked as they climbed on board.

"Uh . . . yeah," Sky muttered. She sighed as the five of them walked down the aisle and piled into the backseat. "I was just doing some thinking."

"Oh, *that* explains it," Jordan said sarcastically. "I forgot. You can't think and walk at the same time."

Sky decided to ignore that little comment. She shifted in her seat so that her back was to Jordan. That way, he was blocked off from any conversation between Alex, Carrie, and her. This was none of his business, anyway.

"Seriously," she said in a low voice. "I don't think we should go to Amy's this afternoon."

Alex's face soured. "Sky, we already talked—"

"No, really," Sky interrupted. "I think it's a bad idea."

Carrie laughed once. "And it took you *this* long to figure that out?"

"You guys are going to *Amy's* this afternoon?" Jordan suddenly asked. "Amy *Anderson*?"

Sky glared at him over her shoulder. "No."

"Yes, we *are*," Alex stated briskly.

"Cool!" Jordan exclaimed. "Can I come?"

Sky rolled her eyes, then slumped back. This was just great. Why was it that whenever Jordan was around, it was completely impossible to have a serious conversation?

"Hey, Alex, I thought we were going to do some boarding in the parking lot at the mall," Sam said from the end of the seat, sounding vaguely insulted. "Aren't we?"

Alex sighed deeply. "Look, the mall can wait. It's not going anywhere. Amy Anderson invited Carrie, Sky, and me over to watch *Days of Our Lives* with her this afternoon." She gave both Sky and Carrie a long, meaningful look. "And that's what we're going to do."

"Oh," Jordan said quietly. "Well, I guess Sam and I will just entertain ourselves then. You guys have fun."

Now *he* sounded insulted, too. But Sky

figured that might work to her advantage. Maybe Alex might start to feel guilty.

"Amy Anderson's house isn't going anywhere, either, Alex," Sky said. "When she gets on the bus, why don't you just tell her that we already have plans?"

"Because we *don't* have plans," Alex retorted.

Sky gestured toward Sam. "What about skateboarding at the mall?"

"We *always* go to the mall!" Alex cried.

Sky frowned. "No—actually we always go to *my* house."

"Whatever," Alex groaned. "It's always the same thing, day after day. Haven't you guys noticed that nobody ever does the same thing day after day except losers like us?"

Carrie sat up straight. "Excuse me?" she asked.

Alex didn't say anything.

For a moment, the backseat was perfectly quiet. The jumble of voices on the bus sounded very far away. Sky went over the words again in her mind. *Losers like us?*

"Uh . . . what do you mean by that, exactly?" Jordan asked, breaking the silence.

Alex pulled her baseball cap off her head, ran a hand through her hair, then put the cap back on backward. She looked out the window. "Nothing," she mumbled. "Just forget it."

"No way, José," Carrie said. "You said it. Answer the question."

Alex lifted her shoulders, but she didn't reply.

Sky began to squirm in her seat. Was it her imagination or was it suddenly tense in here?

Brick closed the door and started the engine. The bus jumped forward.

"Look, I'm sorry," Alex said finally. "I didn't mean it that way."

"Of course you did," Carrie said. But then she smiled. "Hey—I agree with you. If people who do the same old thing every single day are losers, then The Amys are the biggest losers of all. All they do is sit around and watch *Days of Our Lives*."

Alex laughed.

"You know, maybe you're right, Alex," Carrie added dryly. "Maybe it will be a good experience for us to hang out with some other losers and see what *they* do every day."

"Oh no," Jordan said, shaking his head at Carrie. "Don't tell me *you're* having an identity crisis now, too. . . ."

Sky let out a deep breath and tuned out the rest of the conversation. Relief flooded through her. Carrie always picked the right moment to make a joke out of things. Even if they *were* going to Amy's—and it looked as though they were—at least they weren't fighting.

In the grand scheme of things, that was all Sky really cared about.

Eight

Alex had begun to feel anxious even before she got off the bus. At least Amy hadn't said anything when she, Sky, and Carrie had passed her on their way out the door. Alex had been certain she'd say something that would give away the lie. But Amy had been too involved in conversation with Mel and Aimee to even say good-bye.

It didn't matter much, though. Carrie and Sky were going to find out the truth sooner or later.

As the three of them left Sky's boat and hiked up Pike's Way toward Pacific Drive, Alex's anxiety began to grow. The sky had turned an ominous gray. The pine trees were swaying violently in the wind. Even the *weather* seemed to be telling her that she was making a huge mistake.

By the time they reached Amy's doorstep,

Alex's anxiety had turned to full-blown panic.

It didn't help that Amy's house looked more like a museum than a place where people actually lived. It was huge and white, with these beautiful narrow windows in front. It looked a lot like Carrie's house, in fact. Then again, Carrie's house was just around the corner, on Whidbey Road. Every house in this part of Taylor Haven looked like a museum.

"So here we are," Alex managed to say.

Sky raised her finger to ring the doorbell. Then she stopped. Her hand fell to her side.

"You guys sure you want to do this?" she whispered, glancing at them. "We can still bag the whole thing."

Carrie rolled her eyes, then strode past the two of them and knocked loudly on the door. "We're going in," she said impatiently. "We're *here*, aren't we? Besides, it's going to be funny, remember?"

"Coming!" Amy called from deep inside the house.

Oh, boy, Alex thought. She shifted her feet, gripping her skateboard tightly under

70

her arm. She kept her eyes pinned to her sneakers. She couldn't let Carrie and Sky see how scared she really was. Her palms were sweaty and her heart was rattling like a machine gun.

A moment later the door opened. "Hi, Alex!" Amy sang out. "I'm so glad . . ." Her voice trailed off when her eyes fell on Sky and Carrie.

Alex's insides lurched.

I'm in big, big trouble. . . .

For the briefest instant, Amy looked as if she had just smelled something rotten, like spoiled milk. But then her wide smile reappeared.

"I'm so glad you guys could make it," Amy finished. "Come in, come in. Alex, you can leave your skateboard right out front. The show's about to start."

Sky couldn't help but gape as she walked through the door. This place was even nicer than Carrie's house. The front hall had a marble floor and a big sweeping spiral staircase. An enormous abstract painting hung on the far wall.

"Alex, why don't you head upstairs and tell Aimee and Mel that you guys are here," Amy instructed. "Sky and Carrie can help me get some drinks and snacks from the fridge."

Sky exchanged a quick glance with Carrie. *That* was a weird thing to say. She could tell Carrie was thinking the exact same thing. Usually, when you had guests over—especially guests whom you barely knew—you *asked* them for help. You didn't just assume they would help and talk about them as if they weren't in the room.

"Uh, sure," Alex said hesitantly. She sounded slightly bewildered. "You sure you don't need me to help with anything?"

Amy shook her head. "No, we can manage. Right, guys?"

Guys? Sky looked at Carrie again. Carrie shrugged.

"Right," Sky said. She forced a weak smile. This morning Amy had insulted Carrie. She'd never even apologized. Now, apparently, Carrie was one of the "guys." The whole situation was very, very strange.

"Alex, the TV room is the last room on

the left, at the end of the hall," Amy called.

"Um, okay." Alex began to walk up the spiral staircase with slow, tentative steps.

"So." Amy clasped her hands in front of her. "You guys want to follow me to the kitchen?"

Like everything else in Amy's house, the kitchen was spotless, gigantic, and white. It was about the size of Sky's entire boat. There was a little cutting board island in the middle of the floor and a small table off to one side. Sky stood there with Carrie while Amy rattled around the cupboards, looking for something to eat.

"You know, Carrie," Amy said, "I'm sorry about what I said on the bus this morning. The truth is, I've always admired your taste in clothes. The nice thing about wearing black all the time is that you're never in danger of clashing." She paused. "Plus, you're always ready for a funeral at a moment's notice."

Uh-oh, Sky thought. That probably wasn't the apology Carrie had been looking for.

But Carrie just smirked good-naturedly. "What a coincidence," she said. "I've always admired *your* sense of fashion, too. You're the only person at school who manages to show off her belly button every single day. I feel like I know it as well as my own."

Sky grinned.

"Well, if you didn't pig out so much at lunch, you might feel differently about showing yours," Amy said sweetly.

Sky's grin abruptly vanished.

Carrie frowned. "Excuse me?"

"Nothing. So what do you guys want to eat, anyway?" Amy laughed harshly. "I'd ask you to help yourselves, but with Carrie around, there might not be enough left for the rest of us."

Sky swallowed. Why was Amy being so mean? Carrie wasn't even remotely fat.

"As a matter of fact, I'm not hungry, Amy," Carrie stated flatly. "If you can believe it."

Amy ignored her. "Sky?" she asked. "You want anything?"

Sky shook her head. She didn't trust herself to speak. She might get angry—and the last thing she wanted was to get into a fight.

Amy shrugged, then opened the refrigerator door. "Carrie, I'm curious about something," she said. She pulled out a bottle of diet Coke and put it on a counter. "Don't your parents care about the way you destroy your hair with that black gook? It's so nasty. I know *my* parents would freak."

Sky winced. Was Amy *trying* to start a fight or something? Carrie *hated* talking about her hair almost as much as she hated talking about her parents.

"Do your parents care about the way you treat your guests?" Carrie shot back. Her voice was shaking. Sky could tell that her feelings had been majorly hurt. "I know *my* parents would freak if they found out *I* was the biggest jerk on the planet."

Amy snorted. "Better the biggest jerk than the biggest loser."

Oh no, Sky said to herself. She put her face in her hands. She wished she could be someplace very far away, like in another state—or maybe on another planet.

"You know, I'm sorry," Carrie announced. "I just remembered something. I have to leave. I've got to go home and

alphabetize my underwear drawer. Later."
She stomped into the hall.

Sky hesitated for an instant, then dashed out of the kitchen. "Carrie, wait!" she cried.

But by that time, Carrie was already out the door.

Alex was beginning to get fidgety. *Days of Our Lives* was starting. Soft violin music filled the room. But there was still no sign of Sky, Carrie, and Amy. She'd thought she'd heard someone yelling downstairs. Was everything all right? What was taking them so long?

All at once, Amy burst through the door. She shook her head. Something about the way she looked made Alex very nervous. She looked extremely upset.

"What's up?" Alex asked.

"Alex, I'm sorry," Amy said with a sigh. "Sky and Carrie just took off."

Alex blinked. "What do you mean they took off?"

"They just bolted." She shrugged, then sat down next to Alex on the couch. "We were getting stuff to eat and drink, and Carrie just kind of flipped out on me."

Alex's eyes widened. "Are . . . are you serious?" she stammered.

Amy nodded.

Alex glanced at Aimee and Mel. For the first time all afternoon, they were no longer watching TV. They were watching *her*.

Nobody said a word.

"Flipped out?" Alex finally repeated. Her voice was strained. "Uh . . . What did she do?"

Amy shook her head. "I don't even know. I was asking her about her hair— and then out of the blue, she called me the biggest jerk on the planet."

Alex felt the color draining from her cheeks. She couldn't believe it. Why on earth had Carrie done something like *that*?

"I really don't know what happened," Amy went on. "Everything seemed fine to me."

Alex leaned back against the soft cushions. Her jaw hung open slackly. This was crazy.

Her friends had bolted and she was alone with The Amys.

Who would have thought her first day of

eighth grade was going to turn out like *this?* If someone had described this scene to Alex this morning, she probably would have started cracking up—or made sure that person was comitted to an insane asylum.

"Alex, you don't have to stay if you don't want to," Amy said quietly. "I understand."

Alex nodded. She sat there, gazing at the TV. She thought long and hard. She *could* just get up and leave. But at the very least, *somebody* needed to offer some sort of explanation or apology for Carrie. They were guests here—or they had been, anyway. Still, she wasn't really sure how she was going to answer. She wasn't sure of anything.

Well, that wasn't quite true.

She *was* sure that she had been ditched by her two best friends.

And in spite of the fact she had lied to them, that was still a pretty lame thing to do.

"You know," Alex said, not knowing what she was going to say until the words actually came out of her mouth. "I think I *will* stay."

Nine

"I can't believe that, that, that . . . *jerk*," Carrie spluttered. She paced back and forth in little circles on the street in front of Amy's house. Her jaw was tightly set. Her breath was coming in quick gasps. She felt as if she were going to explode. "Who does Amy Anderson think she is? What am I even *doing* here?"

"I am so sorry, Carrie," Sky said miserably, staring at the asphalt. She shook her head. "Really. I had no idea it was going to be like that."

"It's not *your* fault," Carrie said. She stopped pacing and glared at the house. "It's not even Alex's fault. It's *my* fault. I should have known Amy was going to be such a . . . *ugh*." She threw her hands in the air, too flustered to continue. "Forget it."

Sky anxiously twirled her hair around

her finger. "I wonder what's taking Alex so long," she murmured.

Carrie looked at her, then looked at the house again. What *was* taking Alex so long?

Hopefully Alex was giving Amy a piece of her mind. Hopefully she was trashing the place. That would be perfect. Carrie could just picture Alex methodically taking everything out of Amy's fridge and splattering it all over that disgustingly spotless kitchen.

That would teach Amy not to invite Carrie's friends over anymore.

Alex tried to concentrate on the TV show, but it was useless. *Days of Our Lives* was the kind of stupid show where you couldn't understand a thing unless you had seen the past one hundred episodes. Besides, she was far too agitated to sit still.

"Hey, you guys?" she said, clearing her throat. "I just want to say that I'm really sorry about—"

"Ssh!" Aimee hissed irritably. She was hunched forward, riveted to the man and woman who were arguing on the screen.

"This is *important*."

Alex frowned. Maybe she had made a mistake by sticking around. After all, Amy's friends were just as rude as hers. Maybe she *should* have left.

"Aimee, get a grip," Amy snapped. "*You're* a guest, too, remember?"

"Sorry," she muttered, without much enthusiasm.

Suddenly Amy stood. "Alex, why don't we go to the kitchen and get something to eat? We'll leave these two in peace for a while."

"Uh . . . okay," Alex said. She stumbled to her feet. She *did* want to say something, but for some reason, the thought of being alone with Amy made her feel even more nervous. At least they were going to the kitchen. Maybe if she ate a lot, she wouldn't have to do much talking. She only hoped the Andersons had something edible, like Oreos. There was no telling what they would have to eat in this house.

The seconds kept crawling by in slow motion: *tick . . . tick . . . tick. . . .*

Carrie checked her watch again and

again. *Five* minutes had passed since she and Sky had left, and there was still no sign of Alex. No, more than five minutes had passed. It had been five minutes, forty-four seconds—and still counting. The rain had started. Not only was Carrie getting wet, but a sick feeling was tugging at her stomach. Maybe Alex was using the bathroom or something. . . .

"I don't think she's coming out," Sky said.

Carrie shook her head. "Amy must have told her we left."

"Carrie," Sky began. "I think she wants—"

"She *has* to be coming out," Carrie interrupted. She knew she was trying to convince herself as much as she was trying to convince Sky. "There's no *way* she'd stay in there without us."

Sky opened her mouth again, then closed it before saying anything else. Instead, she simply turned and began plodding down the street in the direction of Whidbey Road, wrapping her arms around herself to keep warm.

"Hey!" Carrie shouted. "Where are you going?"

Sky kept walking. "I'm going to your house, Carrie," she called over the sound of the rain. "There's no point hanging around here anymore, unless you want to get soaked."

Carrie swallowed. "What about Alex?"

"I guess she's decided who she wants to hang out with today," Sky said.

Carrie ran a trembling hand through her damp, dyed black hair. She wanted to argue. She wanted to prove Sky wrong. She was actually angry—at *Sky*. It was totally crazy, but she couldn't help it. Being angry at Sky was better than facing the truth. It was better than accepting the awful truth that Alex was staying . . . in *there*.

She looked at her watch one last time. Raindrops splashed on her wrist. A full *six* minutes had now passed.

"Carrie?" Sky asked. "Are you coming?"

Carrie shook her head. She knew there was no denying it anymore. Alex had clearly made her choice. Her own friends weren't good enough. She was hanging with the painfully cool crowd now.

All the warmth in Carrie's body seemed to slowly drain out the bottom of her feet, leaving her very cold and empty. But there was nothing left to do.

"I'm coming," she said softly. She glanced at the door one last time. "I'm coming."

"What do you feel like?" Amy asked. "Cheese and crackers?"

"Uh . . . whatever you have is fine," Alex said, sitting down at the kitchen table.

Amy paused. "How about some Orange Milano cookies?"

Now they were getting somewhere. Orange Milanos weren't Oreos, but they were a step in the right direction. "Sure," Alex replied.

Amy grabbed the bag of cookies and two plates from another cabinet. Alex couldn't help but notice how *grown-up* Amy was acting. At Sky's house, or her house, or even Carrie's house, they never used plates. They just stood by the refrigerator, stuffing their faces directly from whatever bag or container they had ripped open. Alex's dad would have been proud. Her mom, too, for that matter.

"You know, I don't want to cause any

problems between you and your friends," Amy said, carefully laying three cookies on each plate.

Alex nodded, keeping her eyes lowered. "I know," she said. "And I'm really sorry about the way Carrie acted. It's just . . . well, I should have told you I was bringing her with me—but, you know, when you said 'you,' I just sort of assumed . . ." Her voice trailed off.

Well, so much for *that* apology. She sounded like an idiot. She immediately crammed a cookie into her mouth.

"I guess that was partially my fault, too," Amy said. She took a delicate bite from one of her Orange Milanos, chewed for a moment, then shrugged. "I *should* have invited her and Skyler when I invited you." She raised her eyebrows. "You three *are* a trio."

Alex glanced up at her. Something about Amy's tone made her uneasy. She sounded as if she were talking to a four-year-old.

"Just like you guys," Alex said, gulping down her mouthful. "Right?"

"*Exactly.*" Amy put her cookie down on the plate and looked Alex in the eye.

"Which is part of the reason I invited you over. I'm tired of being considered part of that same old threesome all the time. I mean, aren't you?"

Alex shrugged. "It's different with us. You guys are The Amys. We're just Sky, Carrie, and Alex." She stuffed the second cookie into her mouth.

"Actually, you and I are a lot alike," Amy said. "That's why these little groups are silly."

"A lot alike?" Alex asked. She couldn't help but laugh. *"How?"*

Amy smiled. "Just in the way that some kids at school look up to us. Like the way they think you're this really cool, hip skater chick. They think that's mysterious."

For a moment, Alex chomped slowly, studying Amy's face. She couldn't believe what she was hearing. "They *do?*" she asked finally.

"Yeah—in the same way that they think being one of The Amys is mysterious," Amy explained. "But the point is, I don't want to be *one* of The Amys anymore. I don't want to be one of *anything*. I don't want to be mysterious . . . or even popular. I just want to be me: Amy Anderson." She leaned back in her chair, looking slightly embarrassed. "Does that make any sense?"

Alex shook her head, but she was smiling. That made a lot of sense. She just wouldn't have expected a comment like that to come from Amy Anderson. It was a pretty cool thing to come out and say, especially to somebody you hardly knew.

"I mean, let's say, for example . . . I wanted to go skateboarding," Amy continued. "People would think I was going crazy. They would be like, 'Can you believe that one of The Amys is going skateboarding? What is she trying to prove?'"

Alex's eyes narrowed. She didn't quite follow. "You want to try *skateboarding*?"

Amy laughed. "No. But the point is, even if I *wanted* to, it's almost like I couldn't. I'm locked into my image as one of The Amys. And The Amys don't skateboard. It would be the same thing if you wanted to *stop* skateboarding. You have your image and I have mine. And a lot of it depends on the people we hang out with all the time."

Alex laughed, too. Amy was absolutely right. In fact, a lot of what she'd said mirrored what everyone had been telling Alex all day. People *would* think Alex was going crazy if she changed the way she dressed or stopped skateboarding. Luckily, there was no danger of that ever happening, but still, it was true.

"Anyway, do you understand what I'm getting at?" Amy asked.

Alex nodded. A little grin formed on her lips. "Definitely. And, hey, if you ever *do* want to go skateboarding, *I* won't tell anyone."

When Carrie and Sky got to Carrie's house, Carrie no longer felt sad or empty or depressed. She just felt enraged.

"That's it," she stated, slamming the door shut behind them. "As of this moment, I am never, ever, ever talking to Alexandra Wagner again."

Sky blinked. "I know it was a lame thing to do, but maybe she had—"

"Don't even *try* it," Carrie stated, cutting her off. She stormed across the peach-and-white checkered floor and into the peach-and-white colored kitchen, leaving wet footprints in her path. "There's no excuse for what she did. None at all."

Sky followed her. "You're upset right now," she said. "You have a right to be. I'm really mad at Alex, too. But—"

"Carrie?" Mrs. Mersel's voice drifted in from the living room. "Is that you, honey?"

Carrie squeezed her eyes shut and groaned. "No, Mom, it's Madonna."

"Hi, Mrs. Mersel," Sky called cheerfully.

"Skyler?" Carrie's mom anwered. "Hi, dear! I'll be right in."

Oh, please . . . Carrie hung her head. This was just great. So on top of everything that had happened today, they were going to finish the afternoon by having a little chat session with her mom.

Mrs. Mersel strolled into the kitchen in all her sleek, suited glory. "Hi, Skyler!" she cried, kissing her on both cheeks. "Oh, look at you! You look so *cute!*"

"Thanks," Sky gushed.

"Mom, we're busy," Carrie moaned. "Can you please just leave us alone?"

Mrs. Mersel looked around the kitchen, as if she hadn't heard. "Where's Alex?" she asked.

Carrie swallowed. "Alex *who?*" she muttered under her breath.

Mrs. Mersel shot a puzzled glance at Sky.

"Uh . . . we're, uh, sort of having a little crisis right now," Sky explained.

"*Exactly,*" Carrie said, raising her voice. "So we'd appreciate a little privacy, okay?"

"Okay, okay." Mrs. Mersel laughed once. "I'm on my way out. It was nice to see you, Skyler."

"You too, Mrs. Mersel," Sky called.

Carrie tugged at her hair. Why did she have the most clueless mom on the planet? She closed the kitchen door, then headed for the freezer and grabbed a big carton of chocolate chip ice cream. Perfect. She tossed the carton onto the kitchen table, grabbed a spoon, and within seconds, she was gobbling as fast as she could.

"Uh . . . Carrie?" Sky said. She sounded nervous. "Are you all right?"

"Not really," she answered dismally. She was too tired to even lie. "You know, it's funny, Sky. You were right. I *can* use our visit with Amy as material for one of my stories. It was definitely more horrifying than anything I could have thought up myself."

The Three Girls on The Hill
A Stupendous Tale of Human Suffering and Torture (Parental Discretion Advised)
By Carrie Mersel

The town of Stony Brook never changed. It had been the same for centuries. It was a small, quiet, almost desolate place, and few outsiders ever moved there.

The old abandoned mansion at the top of the hill towered above everything else. It served as a grim monument to Stony Brook's eccentric ways. Nobody could remember the last time anyone had lived within its bleak stone walls. Behind its dusty windows, there was only blackness.

But then one day, the town of Stony Brook discovered it would never be the same again.

The mansion was no longer empty.

Three strange girls had moved in--girls whom nobody in Stony Brook had ever seen. And within weeks of their arrival, the girls decided to throw a party. It was going to be the biggest party Stony Brook had ever seen. Everyone in town was invited.

The night of the party was a wet and starless one. Rain fell in torrents. The sky was like thick black velvet. People could barely see their way to the mansion— except for when its stark shadow was illuminated by lightning.

Something terrible was going to happen. The people could feel it. . . .

Ten

By the time Alex glided onto Yesler Street, the rain had already stopped. The sun was now a fiery orange ball at the end of the road, barely visible through the clouds hanging just over the Puget Sound horizon. She must have been running later than she thought. Matt was already home from practice. He was in the driveway, shooting baskets at the little hoop nailed above the garage door.

"Where have *you* been?" he asked, dribbling absently. "It's past six."

Alex hopped off her skateboard and stepped on it, flipping it up into her hand. "You wouldn't believe me if I told you," she said.

He sneered, then turned and squared up for a shot. "Try me."

She waited until the ball was just about

to leave his hands, then said, "Amy Anderson's house."

The shot clanged loudly off the rim. She snickered.

"You're right," he said. "I don't believe you."

Alex shrugged, then headed up the front walk. "Hey, did Sky or Carrie call?" she asked.

Matt shook his head. "Not while I was here. But I just got back fifteen minutes ago." He paused and squinted at her. "Were you *really* at Amy Anderson's house?"

"Yeah." Alex grinned. "What's the big deal?"

He blinked a few times. "The big deal is that she's an imbecile."

Mr. Vocabulary, she thought, rolling her eyes. "She's *not* an imbecile," Alex said. "She's not that bad."

"Not that bad," he repeated. "Um, Alex? Did you break into Carrie's parents' liquor cabinet or something? I won't tell Dad."

"That's funny, Matt," she said dryly. "I bet your sense of humor is really gonna take you places in high school." She stopped as she pulled the front door open. "By the way, how *is* high school?"

He shrugged, then picked up the ball and started dribbling again. "Pretty much like being a fifth-grader at Robert Lowell all over again, if you wanna know the truth." He chuckled. "Oh yeah—you'll be happy to know that Mark Sullivan bites compared to some of the older skaters there. So you better start practicing."

"*You're* the one who needs practice, bud," she teased, closing the door behind her. "That jump shot is looking pretty weak."

"Alex?" her dad called from his study.

"Hi, Dad." She slung her book bag off her shoulder and tossed her skateboard into the front hall closet. "How was your day?"

"Fine, fine," he answered. "How was yours?"

She began walking up the stairs. How *was* her day? She didn't quite know how to answer that one. She paused at the top of the stairs. "Did Sky or Carrie call?"

"Nope."

Hmm. She frowned. That was odd.

Maybe Carrie was still too riled up to talk to anyone right now. But she figured Sky would have called—at least to explain why *she* had bolted. Oh, well. She would just have to call them. She pushed open the door to her room.

"Yuck," she muttered.

One of these days, she would definitely have to clean up. Not now, of course—but some day. She carefully tiptoed through the piles of T-shirts and socks and jeans and books, then flopped onto her bed and snatched the phone off her night table. She punched in Carrie's number.

After three long rings, somebody picked up. "Hello?" Carrie anwered.

"Hey," Alex said. "It's me. I just—"

Click.

"Hello?" Alex asked. She wrinkled her brow. "Carrie?"

Nobody answered.

"Carrie?" she asked again.

But Carrie wasn't there. She had hung up.

Wow. Alex's pulse picked up a beat. Carrie must have been pretty mad. *Really* mad. But why would Carrie be mad at *her? She* was the one who should have been mad at Carrie. She reached over and hit the redial button.

Again the phone rang: once, twice, three times.

Come on, Carrie, Alex silently urged. *Just pick up the phone.*

Finally, after the fourth ring, a chirpy voice answered. "Hello?"

"Uh . . . hi, Mrs. Mersel," Alex said hesitantly. "It's Alex. Is Carrie there?"

"Oh, hi, dear," Mrs. Mersel said. She sounded concerned. "Yes, she's here. One moment, please." She covered the mouthpiece. Alex heard the muffled sound of yelling. A few seconds later, Mrs. Mersel got back on the line.

"Carrie's very upset right now, Alex. She doesn't want to come to the phone."

Alex swallowed. "She doesn't?"

"No." Mrs. Mersel paused. "Did you two get into some kind of fight?"

"Uh . . . not that I know of," Alex mumbled. She licked her lips. Her mouth was very dry all of a sudden. "Can you just, um . . . can you please tell her to call me when she gets a chance?"

"I will, dear," she said. "I hope you two work this out."

"Me too," Alex said quietly. "Thanks. Bye."

She pressed the hang-up button and immediately dialed Sky's number. After just one ring, Sky answered. "Hello?"

"Sky—it's me, Alex," she said urgently.

There was no response.

"Sky?" Alex asked.

"I'm busy, Alex," Sky whispered. "I can't talk."

Alex's heart was thumping loudly now. She felt as if her stomach were twisting into a tight knot. "Sky, what is going on?" she whispered. "Are you guys mad at me or something?"

There was another pause. "Look, Alex—if you don't know the answer to that question, I really can't help you."

"But I'm the one who should be mad at *you* guys!" Alex cried. "*You* were the ones who took off!"

"And *you* were the one who stayed," Sky said simply. "I mean, I can't believe you would do that after the way Amy treated Carrie. Look, I really gotta go."

Alex shook her head desperately. "No, Sky, wait—"

"Bye, Alex." There was a sharp *clunk.*

Alex blinked. After a few deep breaths, she reached over and dropped the phone back on the receiver.

This was insane. She had gotten in fights with Carrie before, but things had never gotten to the point where they couldn't even *talk.* And she almost never fought with Sky.

Alex rolled over on her back. A painful lump was building in her throat. Her eyes started to sting. She sniffed once and ran her hand over her face. It came back wet.

She couldn't believe it. She was *crying.* She couldn't even remember the last time she had cried.

Well, one thing was for sure.

If today was any indication of how the rest of her year would turn out, eighth grade was going to stink.

Tuesday:

The Silent Treatment

7:30 A.M. Carrie wakes up and renews her solemn vow not to talk to Alex.

8:23 A.M. Sam gets on the bus and sits in the backseat.

8:25 A.M. Jordan gets on the bus and sits next to Sam.

8:27 A.M. Mel and Aimee get on the bus and sit in the second seat from the front.

8:29 A.M. Alex gets on the bus and sits next to Jordan. Jordan and Sam want to know what happened at Amy's house. Alex tells them that it was terrible. She's having a fight with Carrie and Sky. Before she can fully explain why, Amy gets on board and sits next to her. Alex knows this is *not* going to help fix things with Carrie and Sky.

8:35 A.M. Carrie sits in the front seat. She tries to covince herself that the

100

backseat was never that great, anyway.

8:40 A.M. Sky boards the bus. When she sees that Alex is sitting next to Amy, she nearly shrieks. What is *Amy* doing in *their* backseat? She sits next to Carrie.

9:03 A.M. Alex leaves a note in Carrie's locker:

Hi, Carrie,
  I feel terrible about what happened yesterday. I had no idea you would be so mad. Can we please talk about this? I'll see you at lunch.
                                                    Alex

10:15 A.M. Carrie finds Alex's note and tears it to shreds.

10:55 A.M. Jordan has math with Carrie. He wants to know what's going on, especially why Amy Anderson sat in the backseat. Carrie tells him in no uncertain terms that she's no longer friends with Alex. Alex has chosen to become one of The Amys.

12:03 P.M. Jordan runs into Sam by the boys' lockers and tells him what Carrie said.

12:30 P.M. Alex sits at the usual table. Jordan and Sam are there, but they are strangely quiet. Alex knows Carrie must have talked to them. She tries to explain the situation from her point of view, but before she can finish, The Amys sit at their table. They ignore Jordan and Sam.

12:31 P.M. Carrie stops at the infirmary and complains of stomach pains to avoid going to the cafeteria.

12:32 P.M. Sky stops at the infirmary for the same reason.

12:45 P.M. Jordan excuses himself from the table. Sam follows. They loiter in the hall by the boys' lockers until recess starts. They both agree that it looks as if Alex *is* becoming one of The Amys.

12:50 P.M. Amy asks if she, Aimee, and Mel can come to Alex's house this afternoon. Alex says it's a bad time for her. She needs to clear things up with her friends first.

1:03 P.M. Alex runs into Sam in the courtyard. She asks if he wants to go skateboarding. He says he doesn't feel like it today.

1:45 P.M. Alex sits next to Sky in Ms. Lloyd's English class. Sky refuses to talk to her. Alex scribbles a note and passes it to Sky:

> I need to talk to you. I'm sorry, okay?

1:46 P.M. Sky scribbles a note and passes it to Alex:

> There's nothing to talk about.

1:47 P.M. Ms. Lloyd sees Alex reading the note and loudly informs her that she can amend her social calendar after class.

2:43 P.M. In a fit of near starvation, Sky and Carrie raid Sky's locker and devour her tofu burger and carrot sticks. Carrie doesn't want to ride the bus home this afternoon. She can't deal with seeing Alex or The Amys. She wants to go straight to the mall. She's going to get Jordan and Sam to go with her and Sky.

3:15 P.M. Alex gets on the bus. The backseat is empty. She sits down and is soon joined by Amy, Aimee, and Mel.

3:17 P.M. Sky pokes her head through the door and whispers something to Brick. The bus leaves without her—*and* without Carrie, Jordan, and Sam.

3:22 P.M. As the bus climbs up Pike's Way, Amy asks Alex once again if she, Aimee, and Mel can come over. Alex finally agrees. At this point, she figures, she has nothing left to lose.

Eleven

"So . . . do you guys want anything to eat?" Alex asked, trying her best to sound cheerful. It was pretty difficult, since she felt as though she had a large lead weight sitting in her gut.

"Do you have any Orange Milanos?" Amy asked.

Orange Milanos? "Um, no," Alex mumbled. On top of everything else, she was starting to feel very self-conscious. Again.

Aimee, Mel, and Amy were slouched at the table. All of them were glancing around the Wagners' small, old-fashioned kitchen with dissatisfied faces. Obviously, Alex's house didn't quite measure up to Amy's place.

"We have some Oreos, though," Alex offered.

Amy tossed her blond hair over her shoulder and flashed an empty little smile. "No, thanks. I'm fine, actually."

"Aimee?" Alex asked. "Mel?"

Mel shrugged. "I'm not hungry."

Aimee didn't even answer.

"Well, *I'm* going to have something." Alex grabbed a bag of Oreos from the cupboard and sat in the one remaining empty seat. She immediately began to eat, mostly because she couldn't think of anything to say.

Amy stared at her, wrinkling her nose slightly. "Hungry, Alex?"

"Mm-hmm," she mumbled with her mouth full.

"I see." Amy sighed. "So . . . uh, what does your dad do, anyway? I saw him in the other room."

Alex forced the cookie down her throat. "He's an ad man."

"An ad man?" Amy said. "That's interesting."

Alex looked at her. She didn't *sound* interested. She sounded extremely bored. In fact, she looked as if she'd much rather be somewhere else. So did Mel and Aimee. Mel was staring off into space. Aimee was bent over the table, picking at one of her fingernails.

For a second, Alex was almost tempted

to make up an excuse to get them all out of her house. But, no. She wouldn't give into her angry feelings, like Carrie had. They were here, and she was determined to make this work.

"So, who's your English teacher this year, Amy?" Alex asked.

"Ms. Lloyd," Amy and Aimee both replied at the same time. They looked at each other and laughed.

"We're in the same class, actually," Amy explained.

"Really?" Alex tried to appear excited. "I have her, too. What period?"

"Third," Amy replied.

Aimee held her hands in front of her face, palms down, inspecting her nails. Then she began to pick at them again.

"I have her sixth period," Alex said. "Isn't she a trip?"

Amy frowned. "What do you mean?"

Alex smiled awkwardly. "Well, just the way she looks and all. You know—that hair on her chin."

"Look, can we talk about something else?" Aimee said flatly. "It's kind of gross."

Alex glared at her. Did she always have to be so rude? Alex was just trying to make conversation. If she didn't want to be here, she shouldn't have invited herself over. She was about to share that little thought with her when the door opened.

"Hi," Matt called. "I'm home. Basketball practice got out early today."

All at once, Amy leapt from the table. "Matt!" she cried, dashing out of the kitchen. Aimee and Mel immediately followed. They started giggling.

Alex leaned back in her chair and scowled. Yes, this had definitely been a big mistake. What had she been thinking? Wallowing in misery by herself was much preferable to *this*.

"Hi, guys," Matt said, shooting Alex a dirty look. "I, uh, didn't expect to see *you* here."

There was more giggling.

"Didn't Alex tell you?" Amy squealed. "We're friends now."

Alex started shaking her head. Friends? That was a laugh. Did Amy honestly think they were all *friends*—just because they had hung out in her kitchen for a few hours yesterday? Yeah, they'd had a great conversation, but still . . . if Amy thought they were friends, she didn't know what the word meant.

"That's great, Amy," Matt grumbled. Alex could hear his heavy footsteps on the stairwell. "You guys have fun."

"Well, anyway, we didn't come over to see Alex," Amy said, scrambling after him. "We came over to see you."

Alex's mouth fell open. *Hold on.* Now she *really* couldn't believe what she was hearing. She pushed herself away from the table. The chair screeched loudly on the floor.

"You came over to do *what?*" she barked, marching into the front hall.

The three of them were already halfway up the stairs. Aimee leaned over and whispered something in Mel's ear.

"We want to see your brother," Amy said. She sounded a little confused—not to mention annoyed. "What's wrong with that?"

As if providing a response to that question, Matt slammed the door to his room.

Amy jumped at the sound. She cast one last puzzled glance at Alex. Mel whispered something back to Aimee. The three of them continued up to the second floor.

"Uh—you guys?" Alex said, growing angrier by the second. "Have you considered the possibility that Matt might not want to see *you*?"

"He'll change his mind," Amy replied confidently. She began knocking on his door. Aimee and Mel stood behind her, laughing.

"Oh, Mat-thew," Aimee called in a singsong voice. "We know you're in there. . . ."

Alex found she was quivering with rage. So *that's* why they invited themselves over—to flirt with Matt. It had nothing to do with friendship.

"He has to come out sometime," Amy said quietly, perching herself on the top step. Aimee and Mel settled down on either side of her, their eyes on the door.

Alex couldn't believe it. Carrie had been absolutely right. They *did* have crushes on Matt. Now that he didn't go to Robert Lowell, the only way to get to him was through *her*. That's probably why they had invited her over to watch *Days of Our Lives* in the first place.

All that stuff Amy said about being "locked into my image as one of The Amys" was completely phony. It was all a lie to soften Alex up. And Alex had fallen for it.

The Amys were still calmly sitting at the top of the stairs. They were clearly prepared to wait as long as it took for Matt to leave his room.

Alex clenched her fists at her side. Amy Anderson was the most selfish, scheming, spoiled *brat* Alex had ever met in her entire life. Not only was she chasing after Alex's own brother, but she had ruined Alex's relationship with her four best friends.

Well, there was no point in hanging around here anymore. Alex had made the biggest mistake of her life yesterday. And now she needed to fix it. *Immediately.*

Without another word, she grabbed her skateboard from the front closet and took to the street. The four of them were sure to wind up at Sky's boat sooner or later. And Alex would wait for them there if it took all night.

Skyler Foley's Secret Confession

I admit that I was really angry at Alex at first. I'm still angry. She should have never stayed in Amy's house. She should have never let Amy sit in the backseat of the bus, either. That backseat is <u>ours.</u> Not to get sentimental or anything, but that backseat has belonged to the three of us since the very first day we started at Robert Lowell Middle School. Amy had no business sitting back there. None at all.

But do we have to give Alex the silent treatment?

It isn't really <u>doing</u> anything, except making all of us feel totally miserable. Alex is obviously a wreck. Today in English, she looked like she was going to start crying.

I don't think Carrie feels any better, either. She didn't smile or crack a joke once all day.

Besides, if we <u>don't</u> talk to Alex, we'll

probably end up going to the infirmary at lunchtime every single day for the rest of the year. I can't keep that up. I was about to _die_ from hunger.

Anyway, I think that once Carrie settles down a little bit, I'm going to try to convince her to let Alex tell her side of the story. But I'm curious. There has to be a reason Alex did what she did. I mean, I thought _I_ was at least partially responsible for getting us into this mess, too.

I guess I just want everything to be back to normal.

Twelve

Carrie's shins were starting to ache from all the pounding on the pavement. That was the *last* time she would ever go to the mall without making sure she had a ride home first. None of them had really been in the mood to hang out at the mall, anyway—not even Sky. They were all too depressed.

So after just half an hour of sitting in the food court, they decided to walk back to Taylor Haven—all the way through Ocean's View, back past school, and up Pike's Way.

The walk had taken almost an hour.

And the worst part about it was that they were only at the dock in front of Sky's boat.

Carrie shook her head. The rest of Pike's Way loomed before her. Late afternoon sunlight slanted through the pine trees, casting long shadows across the road. It was all up-hill. It had never looked so steep in her life.

For the first time ever, she actually wished she had listened to her mom and memorized her new cell phone number. If she'd done that, she probably could have gotten picked up.

"I don't think I can make it," she panted.

"What about *us?*" Jordan asked, waving his arm listlessly at Sam. "You're just at the top of the hill. We're a whole other mile past *that.*"

"Uh . . . do you guys want to stop in for a drink or something?" Sky asked. "I bet my mom will be home soon. She might be able to give you guys a ride."

Carrie managed a tired grin. "*Might* be able to?"

Sky shrugged. "It depends on—"

"Hey, look!" Sam suddenly yelled. "Isn't that Alex?"

Carrie whirled around. Sure enough, someone on a skateboard was cresting over the top of the hill and speeding toward them. Someone wearing a backward green baseball cap.

"That *is* Alex," Sky said.

The four of them looked at each other.

Panic instantly seized Carrie. Her mind started racing. She supposed they could just make a run for the boat. . . .

"Maybe we should talk to her," Sky said quietly.

"*No,*" Carrie said. They were definitely *not* going to talk to her. If they talked to her, she might try to offer some kind of excuse for what she had done—and knowing them, they might just buy it. But there *was* no excuse. None.

"Come on, Carrie," Sky said in a pleading tone. We can't—"

"Forget it," Carrie snapped. "Nothing can change the fact that she ditched us for The Amys. If *you* guys want to let her try to talk her way out of that one, be my guest." The words tumbled out of her mouth in a rush. "*I'm* going inside."

She made a hasty beeline for the dock.

"Carrie, *wait,*" Sky called after her.

Carrie stopped and turned around. "Come *on,*" she commanded.

But it was too late. Alex was swerving across the road in a broad, sweeping arc to slow herself down, then she skidded to stop and kicked her skateboard up into her hands.

"I'm *so* glad I found you guys," she gasped breathlessly. "I need—"

"We've got nothing to say to you," Carrie interrupted.

"Carrie, *please*," Alex begged. "Just let me say one thing, okay?"

Carrie shook her head. "No way. You said plenty when you let Amy sit in our seat this morning. I guess there wasn't enough room for *losers* like us, right?" She looked at the others. They were all glancing apprehensively between her and Alex.

"Right?" she repeated.

None of them said anything.

"Carrie—I'm *sorry*," Alex cried. Her voice cracked. She took a step toward the dock.

For a second, Carrie was struck by how awful Alex looked. Her face was flushed and her eyes were puffy and sagging, as if she'd been crying. For a fleeting moment, Carrie wanted to reach out and comfort her. But she resisted.

"I'm going inside," Carrie stated as evenly as she could. "You guys can come with me if you want. . . ."

With that, she strode down the length of

the dock and shut the houseboat door behind her. For a moment, she stood there in the main cabin, facing Puget Sound. She was shaking. She held her breath and listened for any sound on the dock.

A few seconds later she heard footsteps. She couldn't tell how many, though—three pairs or four pairs. . . .

The door opened. Jordan, Sam, and Sky filed into the room.

Alex wasn't with them.

Carrie swallowed. "What happened?" she asked.

Sky shrugged. "She, uh, just left," she said in a hollow voice. "She didn't even say anything else. She started crying. Then she just hopped on her skateboard and started back up the hill."

Carrie looked at Jordan. He looked at the floor.

"So, there's no way you're even going to let Alex tell her side of the story?" Sky asked. "You're just going to keep blowing her off for the rest of your life?"

Carrie opened her mouth, but no words came.

Sam just shook his head. "Well, you don't have to worry, anyway," he said quietly. "I think Alex got the message."

Carrie didn't answer. She was expecting to feel relieved that Alex had gotten the message. She *didn't* want to hear Alex's side of the story.

But the truth of it was that she felt a whole lot worse than she felt before.

<u>Alex Wagner's Book of Deep Thoughts</u>

<u>Entry 3</u>

So much for trying to fix my mistakes. I ended up losing everything. I guess that's what I get for being stupid. That's what I get for worrying about incredibly dumb things like being a "<u>girl</u> girl" —or being a loser because I do the same thing all the time with the same people.

I have a feeling I won't have to worry about <u>that</u> anymore, though. The "same people" want nothing to do with me.

One good thing happened, at least. Amy, Mel, and Aimee never made it into Matt's room.

They were gone by the time I got home. Dad threw them out of the house. He was pretty mad, actually. I guess all their giggling was pretty distracting while he was trying to work.

When I read what I wrote yesterday, it makes me ill. Needless to say, I added The Amys to the "Things I Hate About School" list. I can't believe I ever thought Amy Anderson could make my life better in any way. I can't believe I actually compared her to my mom. In a way, that's the worst thing of all. It's like I somehow dishonored my mom's memory or something. Mom—if you can hear me, believe me, you're nothing like Amy Anderson.

Anyway, I told Dad he doesn't have to worry about being bothered anymore. That was the <u>last</u> time Amy, Mel, and Aimee would ever be coming over—at least if I could help it.

I guess it's the last time anybody will be coming over for a little while.

It's weird I thought that Sam would have listened to me, at least. He's not usually somebody who lets other people make decisions for him. I thought he would give me the benefit of the doubt. But he just gave me this strange look. Then, of course, he followed Sky and Jordan into the boat.

So I don't even have anyone to skateboard with anymore.

Nope. I don't have anyone.

All I have is me.

So, who's the real loser in this scenario?

Thirteen

Alex had never dreaded anything more than seeing the bus turn onto Yesler Street at that moment. Standing there in front of her house, all by herself, was probably the loneliest she had ever felt in her life.

The bus rolled to a stop beside her. Brick opened the door and gave her his usual, easygoing smile. For some reason, that made her feel even *worse*. He was probably the closest thing she had to a friend on that entire bus. And that was pretty depressing.

"Man—everybody's moving so *slow* today," Brick said. He squinted out the windshield. "There must be something in the air. . . ."

"Sorry," Alex said. She forced herself to climb on board. Then she took a look down the aisle.

For some reason, Jordan and Sam

weren't sitting in the back. They had switched places with Mel and Aimee.

So there were three options, Alex realized. She could sit in the front seat, right in front of Jordan and Sam. Or she could sit in the very back with Mel and Aimee. Or she could sit with someone she hardly knew.

None of those options were very appealing.

Mel and Aimee waved at her.

Alex sneered. Well, she definitely wasn't going to sit with them. They were probably just trying to lure her back there so they could yell at her for ditching them yesterday. She didn't even want to *look* at them. She didn't want to look at anyone, in fact. She plopped down into the front seat and sat with her back rigid, facing forward.

"Wow—it's like musical chairs in here," Brick said.

More like musical friends, she thought dismally.

Brick snapped on the radio as he pulled away from the curb. The tinny sound of some heavy metal song trickled out of the speaker. He began drumming his hands on the steering wheel and mumbling in time to the music. *Boom cha. Boom-boom cha. Boom cha . . .*

Alex's ears perked up. There was a hissing noise behind her. Sam was saying something. Was he talking to her? Was the silent treatment over?

"Hey—you know what I was thinking?" he whispered. "Doesn't Brick totally remind you of the bus driver from the *Simpsons*?"

"Otto?" Jordan breathed. "Yeah."

"He even *sounds* like him." Sam raised his voice slightly and added a rasp, speaking in a dead-on impersonation of Otto. " 'Hey, little dudes!' "

No, Sam *wasn't* talking to her.

A sickening emptiness enveloped Alex at that moment. Sam was joking around with Jordan. It was as if she wasn't even there. Somehow, that made her feel ten times more lonely than she'd felt when she'd been standing alone in front of the house.

She leaned back in her seat. For a few minutes, she seriously debated whether or not to just turn around and demand to know why *they* were giving her the silent treatment, as

124

well. This had nothing to do with them. But in the end, she just couldn't muster enough energy to move, let alone speak.

Suddenly, her body tensed. They were turning onto Pacific Drive. The bus rolled to a stop in front of Amy Anderson's house.

A moment later, Amy climbed on board. She was smiling, as if nothing had happened. The mere *sight* of her was enough to send Alex into a rage. . . .

Amy sat down next to her. And she was *still* smiling.

"What's up, Alex?" she said as casually as ever.

Alex was too infuriated to respond.

"Hey—sorry if we caused any problems with your dad yesterday." She flashed a little smile. "Do you think the next time we come over we could arrange it so he won't be there? I mean, not to complain or anything—"

"The *next* time?" Alex hissed, cutting her off.

Amy frowned. "What?" She looked confused. "What's the matter?"

"The matter? The matter is that you ruined my life. Let me tell you something. You don't have to bother wasting your time stalking Matt." Her voice rose steadily until it was almost a shout. "He's *not* interested!"

Amy's jaw dropped.

Alex found she was breathing hard. Her face was hot. She was dimly aware that everyone on the bus was staring at her, but she didn't care.

"Alex," Amy whispered threateningly. "You want to quiet down?"

"Quiet down?" Alex yelled. "Why *should* I? *You* didn't quiet down! You made so much noise sitting in front of my brother's room that my dad couldn't even work!"

Amy's eyes widened.

The bus slowed and stopped. Brick opened the door and turned around in his seat. "Hey, look, Alex, maybe you should just chill out, okay?" he said gently.

Alex shook her head. She snatched up her book bag and skateboard and stood. "I am *not* going to chill out," she stated.

She looked down the length of the aisle. Every single pair of eyes was glued to her. She took a deep breath.

"I just want everyone here to know that Amy Anderson is in love with my brother,

Matt Wagner," she announced. "You hear that? She's in love with my brother and actually believes he could ever be interested in her. But he thinks she's just a stupid eighth-grader. The word he used to describe her—and I quote—was 'imbecile.' So beware: If Amy invites herself over, it's only to get at your older brothers."

Sam and Jordan started laughing.

Alex shot one more ferocious look at Amy, then turned and headed out the door.

She nearly slammed into Carrie at the bottom of the stairs. She hadn't even noticed that the bus had stopped in front of Carrie's house.

Carrie didn't say anything. Alex didn't know how much she had heard, but it had clearly been enough to send her into a state of shock. Her eyes were bulging.

"Hey—where are you going?" Brick called.

"I'm skateboarding the rest of the way," Alex replied without bothering to look over her shoulder. She laughed grimly. "It's all downhill from here, anyway."

Fourteen

Carrie slowly climbed onto the bus, still reeling from what happened. She'd never seen Alex go off on someone like that before. Something bad had obviously happened between her and Amy yesterday—but what? Something to do with Matt . . .

"If Amy invites herself over, it's only to get at your older brothers."

"Hey, is Alex gonna be all right?" Brick asked nervously. "Maybe I should try to pick her up. I *am* kinda responsible for her."

"She'll be fine," Carrie said distractedly. "She's probably safer on a skateboard—"

"This is all *your* fault," Amy spat.

Carrie glanced at her. Her face was shriveled and bright red. She looked completely embarrassed—and Carrie couldn't have been happier.

"Hi, Amy," she said brightly.

"Don't 'Hi Amy' *me*," she snapped. "You know exactly what I'm talking about."

Carrie smiled as serenely as possible. "I do?"

"Yes you do, *Carrie*. You obviously planted some stupid idea in Alex's head that I'm in love with Matt. That's what made her freak out."

"I don't understand." Carrie pretended to be confused. "You *are* in love with Matt, aren't you?"

Everyone in the bus started cracking up.

Amy's eyes narrowed.

"Carrie, you're gonna have to sit down," Brick said. "We need to get going."

"She can sit *here*," Amy said, pushing herself up in a huff. "I'm going to sit back there, with my *friends*."

"Oh, goody," Carrie said. "That way, we'll keep the foul odor of evil confined to the back of the bus."

Amy paused. Her face was only inches from Carrie's. "You're going to regret saying that," she whispered.

"Yikes!" Carrie cried sarcastically.

Amy stormed to the backseat.

Carrie rolled her eyes and flopped down in front. "Whew," she said, glancing back at Jordan and Sam. She laughed once. "What a way to start your morning, huh?"

"Yeah," Sam said, stone-faced. "I guess Alex is probably feeling the same way, too."

Carrie winced. He might as well have splashed a bucket of cold water over her head. She hadn't even *thought* about that.

"I . . . uh, guess you're right," she mumbled.

"So what are you gonna do about it?" he asked.

Carrie shifted in her seat. She didn't answer for a long time. She'd made up her mind never to talk to Alex again. And she'd meant what she said yesterday: Nothing could change the fact that Alex ditched her for The Amys. But maybe there *was* a good reason. After all, there had to be a good reason for the way Alex had acted just now. Nobody had ever made a fool out of Amy in front of the entire bus and then just stormed off.

"Well?" Sam demanded.

Carrie hesitated. Out of the corner of

her eye, she caught a glimpse of Alex, skateboarding far behind the bus. She looked so *small* from up here. Small and slow and all alone. But she had stood up to The Amys. And that was a very, very cool thing to do.

"She deserves to explain herself," Sam said. "We owe her that much. *I'm* not even mad at her."

Carrie sighed as the bus rolled to a stop in front of Sky's house. "You're right. We do owe her that much. We'll wait for her on the front steps."

Fifteen

Alex was taking a lot longer than anyone had expected. But Sky insisted that the four of them wait until Alex arrived. The first bell had already rung. Sky didn't care. She wasn't going to let Carrie change her mind. They needed to talk to Alex—*now*. Besides, this was much more important than the first five minutes of math or whatever other classes they were missing. This was serious.

"So what *really* happened anyway, exactly?" Sky asked for the third time. "She just freaked out?"

"*Yes*," Jordan said impatiently. He kept glancing toward the front door. "How many times do we have to tell you?"

Sky frowned. It figured that *she* had missed the most exciting thing that had ever happened on Bus #4.

"Look." Sam stood up. "This is really

between you guys, all right? I don't want to be late for class. *I* have no problems with Alex. I'm gonna talk to her myself later." He headed for the door.

Jordan got to his feet. "Me too," he said, following after Sam.

Sky opened her mouth, but Sam and Jordan were already inside before she could say anything.

She glanced at Carrie.

"Don't worry," Carrie said. "*I'm* not going anywhere. I'll be here for however long it takes."

Sky turned back to the road. She propped her elbows on her knees and rested her chin in the palms of her hands, surveying the road. *Hurry up, Alex. We can't wait forever—*

"*There* she is," Carrie said.

Sure enough, the silhouette of a lone figure on a skateboard had turned off Pike's Way.

Sky watched quietly as Alex pushed herself up the road to the little semicircular drive in front of school.

Nobody said a word. Alex hopped off

133

her skateboard. For a moment, it seemed as if they were all waiting for someone else to start speaking.

"I'm really, really sorry," Alex blurted, shattering the silence. "I acted like a total jerk."

Sky drew in her breath. She didn't think she'd ever felt more relieved in her whole life. "I'm sorry, too," she said. "Really. You're not the only one who's been a jerk. We all have."

Alex shook her head. "No. You guys have a total right to be mad," she said. "I should have jumped and left the second you guys did." She groaned. "I can't *believe* I stayed."

"So . . . why *did* you stay?" Carrie asked.

"I thought I should apologize for the way you acted," Alex explained. "I thought that you took things way too far. That's what I *thought*." Her jaw tightened. "Now I know that you did the right thing. *I* was wrong."

"But why did you think that I took things too far?" Carrie asked. "I mean, do you even know what Amy *said* to me?"

Alex looked at the ground. "The only thing she told me was that you said she was the biggest jerk on the planet, then flipped out and left," she muttered.

Carrie laughed miserably. "I guess she left out the part about what *she* said."

"Uh . . . what did she say?" Alex asked, glancing nervously at Sky.

Carrie shrugged. "Only that I pig out at lunch and have nasty black gook in my hair and I'm the biggest loser on the planet."

Alex turned slightly pink. "Carrie—I had no idea. I'm so sorry. I had no idea about *anything*. Look, the only reason she wanted to be friends with me was so she could have an excuse to come over and flirt with Matt."

Sky began twirling her hair around her finger. "So . . . uh, what happened with Matt, anyway?"

Alex looked at the ground. "They invited themselves over yesterday," she explained ashamedly. "It was so lame. All three of them sat at my kitchen table, complaining and picking their nails until Matt came home. Then they chased him up the stairs. Luckily, he locked his door in the nick of time. If my dad hadn't kicked them out, Amy would probably still be there, trying to pick the lock right now."

Sky looked at Carrie.

Carrie started laughing.

Sky started laughing, too. She couldn't help it. The thought of Amy Anderson alone at Alex's, desperately trying to get into Matt's room . . . It was too much.

Pretty soon, all three of them were in hysterics.

Finally, Carrie took a deep breath. "I knew it," she said. "It had to be *something*. I just knew it."

Alex sighed. "Carrie, I'm so sorry. . . ."

"I know, I know," Carrie said. She began pacing agitatedly around the front steps. "It's just that—well, why did you feel like you had to stick around and apologize for *me*? I could have done that myself. *If* it was necessary."

Alex hung her head. The bill of her backward baseball cap pointed sraight up. "I know. I'm sorry. When you're right, you're right. And you were right about Amy."

"*That's* why I didn't want to go over there," Carrie said. "I knew that Amy didn't want to be friends with any of us. She just had some trick up her sleeve. We should have figured out that it had to do with Matt right at the beginning."

Alex just kept nodding. "I know."

"So, does this mean we're all done fighting?" Sky asked hopefully.

Carrie stopped pacing and smirked. "Well, we're *talking*, right?"

"Right." Sky stood. "Let's go to class—"

"Whoa, hold on a second," Carrie said. "We're not done yet."

Sky frowned, but she sat back down. It *sounded* like they were done.

Carrie looked at Alex and folded her arms across her chest. "How come you let Amy sit in *our* seat?" she demanded.

Actually, now that Sky thought about it, Carrie *did* have a point. *Nobody* belonged in their backseat. "Yeah?" Sky asked.

"I had nothing to do with that!" Alex protested, shaking her head. "I swear. *She* sat there, and she wouldn't leave. There was nothing I could do about it."

Carrie paused. "Well, okay. But you have to promise us one thing," she said.

Alex nodded. "Anything."

"Never, ever let anyone besides us sit in the backseat." Carrie grinned. "Even if you have to forcibly remove them. That seat is like . . ." She paused and thought for a second. "Well, it's like the Jordan-Sam-Alex-Sky-Carrie memorial. It's got history. And nobody else belongs."

A smile broke on Alex's face. "You got it."

"And never, ever let anyone else sit at our lunch table, either," Sky added. "The lunch table is the same. It's for us, and us alone. Deal?"

"Deal," Alex stated.

Sky stood up again. "*Now* we can go to class."

"Yeah," Carrie said. Then she hesitated one last time. "Hey—does Matt have a TV in his room?" she suddenly asked.

"Yeah." Alex looked confused. "Why?"

"*Duh*," Carrie said. She smiled mischievously. "Maybe we were wrong. Maybe they were just trying to get in there to watch *Days of Our Lives*."

Sixteen

Alex was just outside the cafeteria doors in front of the boys' lockers when she heard the sound she knew she'd hear sooner or later: the sound of Amy's voice.

"Alex! Stop! I need to talk to you!"

Oh, well. At least Alex had made it to lunch without bumping into her. But she was well aware that it would only be a matter of time before Amy tracked her down.

"What were you *thinking* this morning?" Amy demanded.

Alex turned around. "I just thought everyone had a right to know how rude you are," she explained camly.

"Alex—in case you don't remember, *you're* the rude one. You left me in your house without even saying good-bye. But I let that slide, because I *thought* we were friends."

Alex opened her mouth, but Amy kept right on talking.

"Do you have any understanding of common courtesy?" she continued. "And as if that's not bad enough, your dad comes up the stairs in his flannel shirt and behaves like a total maniac, telling me that—"

"Wait a second," Alex growled. "That house is my dad's *office*. And you were stalking my brother. That made it a little hard for my dad to concentrate on his work."

Amy shook her head. "So what do you have to say for yourself?" she asked, as if she hadn't heard a word Alex had just said.

Alex looked her in the eye. "Just this," she hissed. "If you ever, ever set foot in my house again, you can be sure that my dad will be the *least* of your problems." And with that, she stormed into the cafeteria.

Even from the other end of the long hall, Carrie could see that something had been stuck to her locker—a sheet of notebook paper that stood out in sharp contrast to the locker's bright red paint.

Oh, jeez, she thought, groaning. *What now?*

Judging from the way people were snickering and whispering to each other as they passed by her, it was probably some sort of stupid insult. And she could just guess who was responsible.

As she drew closer, she saw that a single word had been written on the piece of paper in black magic marker: LOSER.

Well, well, well. Wasn't that funny.

Carrie was almost tempted to leave it up there. Or maybe write the words, "Amy Anderson is a . . ." above it. But no, that would be too easy. If Amy actually thought that this was going to make Carrie the slightest bit mad—or even bother her at all—she was sadly mistaken.

Carrie laughed once. She tore the paper off her locker and folded it carefully, sticking it into the pocket of her black skirt.

This lame little prank *did* accomplish one thing, though. Carrie's mind was now made up. It was time for revenge.

Sky hated sitting alone at the lunch table. There was nothing worse than staring at four empty seats, especially when you were surrounded by tables filled with kids who were laughing, talking, and probably wondering why you suddenly had no friends. Sky was considering crawling under her chair with her homemade veggie burrito, when Alex and Carrie entered from the two opposite sets of double doors.

Whew.

They marched directly to the table without even bothering to pick up their trays.

They looked mad.

Uh-oh.

"Uh . . . hey, guys," Sky said nervously as they sat down. "What's up?"

"Something's gotta be done about Amy," Alex announced.

Carrie nodded. "I assume you saw this?" she asked. She reached into her pocket and pulled out a folded piece of notebook paper, then flattened it out on the table.

The word *loser* was written on it in black magic marker.

Sky shot a confused glance at Alex. "Uh, no," she said. "What *is* it?"

"Somebody taped this to my locker this morning," Carrie said. "You didn't see it?"

Sky shook her head.

"Amy must have put it there just now—right before I spoke to her," Alex said.

"You *spoke* to her?" Sky asked, stunned.

"Yup," Alex answered flatly. "She told me that my father was a maniac. Also, she doesn't like the way he dresses."

"Oh." Sky nodded. Now she understood why Alex was so angry.

Sky had learned long ago that every single person besides her in the world had one sore spot—one line that, if crossed, would turn that person into a raging lunatic. With Carrie, it was any crack aimed at her hair. With Alex, it was any crack aimed at her family.

"So, there's only one thing left to do," Carrie said with a devious smile.

"Exactly," Alex said.

Sky blinked. "Uh . . . what's that?"

Carrie and Alex answered at the exact same moment. "Get even," they said.

Seventeen

Alex sat on her bed, staring absently at the wall. Sky sat at the desk. Carrie had managed to shove aside enough of the mess to sit on the floor.

Nobody said anything. Nobody had uttered a sound for the past ten minutes. They were all too busy thinking.

Their revenge on Amy Anderson had to be *genius*.

"You know, it would be really good if we could get Matt involved," Carrie said distractedly. "I mean, in a way, he kind of started the whole thing. If Amy didn't have a crush on him, none of this would have happened."

Alex shook her head. "It *would* be good, but Matt would never go along with one of our plans," she grumbled. "He thinks he's way too mature for stuff like that."

"Well, what if we just make Amy *think*

144

he's involved?" Sky asked. She sat up straight. "I mean, what if we sent her a letter . . . from *him?*"

Alex grinned. That wasn't such a bad idea, actually. The only problem was that none of them could copy Matt's handwriting. Then again, Amy didn't know what Matt's handwriting looked like in the first place.

"That's good, but it would be tough to pull off," Carrie said. "She'd probably suspect it was us. Plus, I really want to *humiliate* her. Publicly."

Alex nodded. Public humiliation was definitely essential. If only she had video taped Amy trying to get Matt to open his door, then she could broadcast it over the Internet for the entire world to see. . . .

Hmm. The Internet. A thought suddenly occurred to her. There *was* a way they could send Amy a message and have her think it was from Matt. They could E-mail her from Matt's computer. He and Alex shared an E-mail address, but it was in Matt's name.

"Uh-oh," Sky teased. "Alex has that *look.*"

Alex sat up. "I was just thinking. We could send Amy an E-mail tonight from

Matt's computer. That way, she would definitely think it was from Matt."

Sky raised her eyebrows. "Do you know Amy's E-mail address?"

"No, but we could send it to one of those school bulletin boards. I know Amy checks those all the time. The Amys use them for gossip."

Carrie began nodding. "Yeah . . . that's good. Normally, I have a moral objection to computers, but in this case . . ."

"We can make it seem like he's apologizing to her," Sky said. "Like he wants to make it up to her somehow . . ."

"Yeah!" Carrie said. She seemed to be growing more excited by the second. "It can even be an invitation to meet him somewhere. Then she'll show up—and *whoops*. No Matt."

"How about the mall?" Sky suggested.

Alex rolled her eyes. "You're just looking for an excuse to go to the mall, Sky."

Carrie shook her head. "No, I think Sky has a point. The mall is a *very* public place. Tons of people go there after school."

Alex nodded. "That's true. But there

should be something more. There needs to be one last detail that makes it perfect."

"You're right," Carrie agreed. "And I think I know what it is. Photographic evidence."

Alex smiled.

"Yup," Carrie went on. "We take Polaroids. Then we tape them to her locker. An eye for an eye, right?"

"*Now* we're getting somewhere," Alex said.

"I've got an even *better* idea," Sky said. "In the E-mail, Matt can tell her that he really likes her, but he hates the way she dresses. He asks her to wear something totally ridiculous."

Alex clapped her hands. "Perfect!"

At once, Carrie hopped off the floor. "How about something like *this*," she said, gesturing at her own long black skirt.

Sky got to her feet. "Perfect."

Alex was the last one to get up. She glanced at the clock on her bureau. "We'd better hurry. It's almost six. Matt'll be home any minute now."

Without another word, the three of them

bolted down the hall and into Matt's room. Alex sat down at his desk and flipped on the computer. Sky and Carrie stood over her while she began typing:

Hi, Amy,

Sorry about the way my father acted yesterday. I didn't want to tell you this in front of Alex, but I *was* glad that you came over to see me. Anyway, I'd like a chance to apologize for what happened in person. Meet me at the food court at Ocean's Edge Mall tomorrow at five. You don't have to respond. Just be there.

                    Matt

P.S. I was thinking, you'd look totally hot in black. You know, the way Carrie Mersel dresses. Not that she even comes close to comparing to you or anything. Would you wear all black for me? Please?

Thursday:

The Plan Unfolds

8:32 A.M. Amy sticks out her tongue at Carrie when Carrie gets on the bus.

11:31 A.M. Alex sees Amy checking the school's computer bulletin board.

12:17 P.M. Alex, Carrie, and Sky notice that Amy looks disgustingly pleased with herself when she walks into the cafeteria.

3:15 P.M. Amy, Carrie, and Sky hear Amy humming to herself outside as they get on the bus to go home.

3:23 P.M. Carrie and Sky get off at Sky's place. Sky grabs some Scotch tape and asks her mom for a ride to the mall.

3:39 P.M. Alex gets her dad's Polaroid camera and skateboards to Sky's place, where Sky's mom, Sky, and Carrie are all waiting in the Foley's old beat-up VW van.

4:11 P.M. Alex, Carrie, and Sky promptly begin stuffing themselves with french fries at the food court. Luckily, french fries are the one *normal* item of food that Sky eats.

4:47 P.M. Alex, Carrie, and Sky position themselves behind the fountain near the food court and await Amy's arrival.

5:07 P.M. Amy appears at the food court. Alex, Carrie, and Sky nearly lose control of themselves. Amy is wearing a long black skirt, a black turtleneck, and black lipstick. A few people from Robert Lowell who happen to be in the food court stare at her.

5:08 P.M. As Amy sits at a table and reapplies her lipstick, Alex snaps three photos.

5:09 P.M. An image forms on the first picture. It's perfect. Amy is sitting there with her mouth open, the black lipstick is clearly visible.

5:10 P.M. Alex, Carrie, and Sky exit the mall and head straight for Robert Lowell. The building is deserted, of course, except for the basketball team practicing in the gym.

5:35 P.M. Sky tapes the photo to Amy's locker. Above it, Carrie tapes a piece of paper with the following inscription: Amy Anderson: Carrie Mersel Wanna-be.

<u>Alex Wagner's Book of Deep Thoughts</u>

<u>Entry 4</u>

I must say, there's nothing quite like perfection.

Perfection, you ask?

Well, yes. Amy's probably still at the mall waiting for Matt.

As corny as it sounds, I think the best part of our little scheme was how we came together as a team. It was truly <u>magnificent</u>. (Oh no. That sounds like a word Matt would use.) But it's true. Carrie's brains, Sky's fashion tips, and my . . . well, computer, I guess all meshed like pieces of a puzzle. I can't wait to see Amy's reaction when every single person at Robert Lowell sees that photo on her locker tomorrow morning.

I guess I should expect the worst. I have a feeling things are going to get really, really ugly between The Amys and us before they get better. And I'm looking forward to it.

The only thing I still kind of regret is that I never told Carrie and Sky that I lied to them. And if I hadn't lied, none of this probably would have happened in the first place. But there's still time. Now that we've made up, I have the rest of my life to tell them. And I definitely will. Someday.

You know, it's funny. I haven't even <u>thought</u> about all that stupid "<u>girl</u> girl" stuff since Tuesday.

So I think my eighth-grade year is going to turn out just fine, after all.